SKULL GOLD

A SHAWN STARBUCK WESTERN

SKULL GOLD

RAY HOGAN

THORNDIKE
CHIVERS

This Large Print edition is published by Thorndike Press, Waterville, Maine, USA and by BBC Audiobooks Ltd, Bath, England.
Thorndike Press, a part of Gale, Cengage Learning.

The text of this Large Print edition is unabridged.
Other aspects of the book may vary from the original edition.
Set in 16 pt. Plantin.
Printed on permanent paper.

LIBRARY OF CONGRESS CATALOGING-IN-PUBLICATION DATA

Hogan, Ray, 1908–
    Skull gold : a Shawn Starbuck western / by Ray Hogan.
      p. cm. — (Thorndike Press large print western)
    ISBN-13: 978-1-4104-0700-9 (alk. paper)
    ISBN-10: 1-4104-0700-4 (alk. paper)
    1. Starbuck, Shawn (Fictitious character) — Fiction. 2. Large type books. I. Title.
PS3558.O3473S55 2008
813'.54—dc22   2008009053

BRITISH LIBRARY CATALOGUING-IN-PUBLICATION DATA AVAILABLE

Published in 2008 in the U.S. by arrangement with Golden West Literary Agency.
Published in 2008 in the U.K. by arrangement with Golden West Literary Agency.

U.K. Hardcover: 978 1 408 41183 4 (Chivers Large Print)
U.K. Softcover: 978 1 408 41184 1 (Camden Large Print)

Printed in the United States of America
1 2 3 4 5 6 7 12 11 10 09 08

SKULL GOLD

1

It was the drumming sound of a fast-running horse that caught Shawn Starbuck's attention. Pulling to a halt in the dry wash he was following, he listened briefly and then abruptly swung the sorrel gelding he rode up the steep slope of the hill to his right and gained the crest.

Again drawing to a stop, he placed his attention on the wide, burnished-looking, heat-seared flat flowing out below. At first he could make out only a swirl of dust on the winding road that cut its way through brush and rock. Then, as the boil of tan and gray drew near, he saw that it was a horse and buggy, that a solitary passenger was on the seat of the rocking, swaying vehicle.

Starbuck frowned. The lone occupant was a woman; but it was no runaway — that was certain. She was leaning forward on the seat, firmly grasping the reins in one hand, now and then applying a long-stocked whip to her galloping horse with the other. It appeared she was simply in a hell of a hurry to leave Wickenburg, only a short distance beyond her.

He searched the desolate stretch of land behind her for pursuers; there were none. Then why the wild haste? There was nothing ahead of her in the way of a settlement but Phoenix, and it was fifty miles or so to the southeast. Surely she was not undertaking such a journey alone — not with Apaches, roving Mexican *bandidos,* and a plentiful supply of outlaws prowling the land. . . . One thing sure, she had better let up on her horse; it would not last long in such heat and at the pace she was forcing.

Starbuck brushed at the sweat beading his forehead. Despite the fact that it was October and only midmorning, the sun, climbing through a cloudless sky, was scouring the land with fierce intensity. He looked again to the onrushing traveler. Although he could recall none along the route he had just covered, it was possible the woman was hurrying to a ranch or homestead somewhere nearby, or more logically, to a mine. There were many pocking the hills around Wickenburg. Like as not she was a miner's wife or daughter, and . . .

He drew up sharply as movement farther

down the road caught at his eye. Raising himself in the stirrups, Shawn cupped a hand over his thick brows, strained to see what it was that had snared his attention. His mouth tightened. . . . Three Apache braves. . . . Evidently they, too, had heard the pound of the running horse and the rattle of the buggy, had paused to investigate. Locating the vehicle with its one passenger, and recognizing easy prey, they had moved in ahead and were waiting.

Starbuck delayed no longer. Roweling the sorrel, he broke off the summit of the hill, started downgrade at a fast run. The buggy was somewhat past his position; he would have to catch up, and to do that his course would be a long tangent across the slope, one that should bring him out even with the racing buggy at about the same point where the braves lay in ambush.

The hillside was rough, given to small washes and scatterings of loose rock and brush clumps. Several times the gelding stumbled or was compelled to veer in his downward flight. Shawn slowed the big horse. The odds for his breaking a leg were too great, and if that happened, he would not only be unable to help the girl, but he would be in serious trouble himself. Accordingly, he altered course, moved for the road on a direct, less hazardous path that would bring him onto it at right angles.

He reached the dusty ribbon, cut into it, spurred the sorrel to a faster gallop. The gelding lengthened his stride, at once began to gain on the reeling buggy, only a hazy outline in the spinning tan cloud ahead.

The separating gap shrank rapidly. Starbuck, bent low over the sorrel's outstretched neck, reached for the forty-five on his left hip. The woman was near the hiding Indians — he'd not overtake her before they closed in.

A rifle shot cracked through the hot air. The braves were springing their trap. Grim, Shawn raked the gelding's flanks with his rowels, felt the horse respond with a burst of speed as they entered a wide, swinging curve.

He could hear the braves yelling, and the shooting was continuing, but the thunder of the sorrel's hooves drowned out all else, and he was unable to tell if the Apaches had been able to stop the girl or not. At the pace she was moving, it was doubtful.

The road straightened before him. A hundred yards ahead he saw the buggy. The woman had driven straight on through the waiting braves, confusing them briefly, but already they had swung about and were racing alongside. One, leaning far over, was endeavoring to grab the headstall of her horse; the others were attempting to ride in close and leap from their ponies into the buggy. The motion of the vehicle as it whipped back and forth was making the dangerous effort not only difficult but nearly impossible.

Starbuck raised his pistol, leveled a shot at the brave nearest him. He was careful, forced to aim well to the side, mindful of hitting the girl should the buggy take a bad lurch.

The bullet missed its target but had immediate effect. Both the Apaches trying to board veered off quickly, began to circle back. Starbuck steadied his weapon over a forearm, pressed off a second bullet at the same brave. The Apache flinched, clutched at his shoulder, changed direction, and rushed off into the brush. Immediately his companion raised the rifle he carried, snapped a shot at Shawn. The bullet was wide, and Starbuck replied with one that caused the man to slow his charge.

The brave trying to halt the buggy had finally succeeded in grasping the horse's bridle and was beginning to pull the black down. He seemed unaware of what was taking place behind him, so intent was he on his task. Starbuck, throwing another shot at the second brave, now pulling off into the nearby hills, again crooked his right elbow, rested his weapon on his forearm and triggered a bullet at the last of the trio. The slug missed the brave, smashed into the head of his pony. The luckless animal collapsed instantly, flung the brave a dozen strides on beyond.

As the pony went down, the black drawing the buggy swerved hard right. The vehicle careened drunkenly, snapped back, jackknifed, and flipped over on its side, throwing the driver to the ground with sickening impact.

Starbuck came off the saddle before the sorrel had even stopped, and ran toward the crumpled figure of the woman. The Apache who had cut for the hills was no longer in sight, and the one thrown from his falling horse, arm hanging at an odd angle from the shoulder, was legging it into the brush. There was no sign of the one he had put a bullet into.

He gave them no further thought, certain he'd seen the last of them, and dropped to his knees beside the motionless girl. Gently turning her onto her back, he felt her throat for pulse. It was there, not strong but fairly regular. He breathed easier, looked closely at her. There was a darkening on the side of her face near the temple where she had struck, and there were a few scratches. Thanks to the mat of grass along the shoulder of the road, she seemed to have no broken bones, but that did not rule out internal injuries, however.

Frowning, he patted her cheek sharply, watching her intently for some indication of reviving. She was young — probably little more than twenty years old, he guessed — and pretty despite the smudges on her face. She was dressed in worn clothing — a man's shirt, pants, and heavy shoes, the kind generally used by miners.

There was no response to his efforts. Rising, he trotted to where the sorrel waited, unhooked his canteen, and returned to her side. Taking his bandanna and soaking it, he mopped at her face and neck. She remained unmoving. Starbuck shook his head. She was hurt worse than he had feared, needed a doctor's attention at once. Best he get her back to Wickenburg as quickly as possible.

Coming upright, he strode to where the little mare she was driving stood trembling between the twisted shafts of the overturned buggy. Grasping the bed of the light vehicle, he tipped it back onto its wheels. A small carpetbag and a half-filled flour sack had also been tossed from the seat when it capsized. The bag had popped open, and appeared filled with clothing; the contents of the flour sack, partially spilled, were made up of food — bread, dried meat, a couple of mason jars of pickled fruit, some coffee beans. Collecting all, Shawn placed them back in the buggy. It would seem that the girl, whoever she might be, had been undertaking a journey to some distant point. Again he reflected on the foolhardiness of such a venture.

Hurriedly straightening out the black mare's harness, Shawn brought up the sorrel, tied him to the rear of the buggy. Then, picking up the unconscious girl, he placed her carefully on the seat. She was limp, nerveless, and if he expected to make the drive to Wickenburg with any speed, he realized he would have to make her secure.

Reaching into his left boot, he obtained the slim-bladed knife he carried, and cutting off a length of rope from his own lariat, he passed it around her slight body and anchored the ends to the braces of the top on her side of the buggy. He drew the rope taut, aware that unless she was pinned tight to the seat there was danger of her being thrown out and suffering more injuries. Should she regain consciousness, she would complain, he knew, at being trussed up so severely, but until then he'd take no chances.

Climbing into the buggy, he settled down beside her. There were still no signs of recovery, but he took time to again bathe her face with the wet bandanna; and then, turning her slim body partly about so that her head might lie on the cushion of the seat back, he laid the cloth upon her forehead.

It was the best he could do for her, and taking up the reins, he swung the black around and started the return trip to Wickenburg. That he could be doing her no favor occurred to him at that moment; she had been fleeing the settlement in great haste, taking with her what possessions she had evidently been able to gather hurriedly. Whatever it was she wanted to leave behind, he would be taking her back to. He shrugged. It was something he could not help; her life depended on receiving medical care.

The mare was tired from the fast run she had just made, and Starbuck disliked the idea of pushing the little horse hard after so short a rest, but there was no other answer. Taking the slack end of the leathers in lieu of the whip, lost when the buggy overturned, he began to slash at the black's rump. Reluctantly, the horse broke into a gallop.

2

Starbuck glanced at the girl. She was stirring weakly, and there was a bit of color in her cheeks. He felt the worry within him lessen; perhaps she wasn't hurt as badly as he'd feared. He continued to study her as the little mare rushed on over the uneven road.

Had she tucked her shoulder-length blond hair up into a hat or cap, he would never have recognized her for a woman when he first caught sight of her. As it was, the thick, cornsilklike tresses were an instantaneous giveaway. She had a wide face with eyes set well apart. He gave a moment's wonder as to their color, decided they were blue most likely. Dark, thick brows, a short turned-up nose, and a full-lipped mouth with complementing firm chin completed her features. Whoever she was, she was most attractive, he thought, and glanced ahead.

Wickenburg was in sight, a dozen or two

houses and business structures scattered loosely about in the low hills. Shawn sighed heavily. It had been a long ride from King Mallory's ranch in the Gila country of New Mexico, and he'd made it almost without a stop, having halted only to rest the sorrel and take a break from the saddle for himself now and then.

But it was worth all the sweat and aches and muscle soreness; Ben was in Wickenburg. This time he would meet his brother, and the long search would end. Ben was working for one of the mines, Jake Wiser, the rider who had told him of Ben, had said, and was living under the name of Damon Friend. Shawn had known of the change of name for some time now, but the fact that Ben was in Wickenburg, working at a steady job, had come as news to him.

It occurred to Shawn only now that he had neglected to ask Wiser just which mine, but that shouldn't pose too large a problem. Evidently it was one of the big operations, and there wouldn't be too many of those in the area.

He would find a doctor first off, however, turn the girl over to him, and then get on about his own business. The town lawman could probably tell him where to find Ben, but if not, he'd ask at one of the saloons;

bartenders were always a source of information. . . . But getting to a doctor was next.

They reached the end of the street, almost like an arroyo as it cut its way between the slopes of adjacent hills, and hurried on toward the first of the houses. He could see people on the boardwalk farther down, where the stores appeared to be concentrated. Like as not the town's physician would have his office there.

The black whirled the buggy around a bend, entered a lane that led directly to the center of the settlement. A man moved into the street from a flower-bordered yard on Starbuck's right, paused to stare at the lathered horse and rocking buggy.

"The doctor!" Shawn yelled. "Where —"

The man seemed momentarily startled and then pointed to a small white house a short distance farther on. Starbuck bobbed his thanks without slowing and rushed on.

There was a wide gate just beyond an aging sign that read DR. P. J. BAILEY, and Shawn swung the buggy through it and onto a graveled drive. Reaching the corner of the house, he drew the black to a halt and leaped to the ground. He heard a door slam as he circled to the opposite side of the buggy and began to tug at the knot in the rope binding the girl to the seat.

"What's the trouble?"

"Accident," Shawn replied without turning. "Buggy tipped over. Hit her head. Wasn't able to bring her to."

Throwing the rope aside, he slid his arms under the girl, lifted her easily from the cushion, and turned.

"You the doc?"

"I am," the man, a squat, balding, middle-aged individual with sharp eyes, answered. He gave the girl a quick glance, added, "Bring her in here."

Starbuck followed him up onto the porch and into the house, the front area of which had been converted into office and waiting room.

"Put her on the examining table," Bailey said, opening a door into quarters in which there were glass cases of medicine, nickeled instruments, and stacks of gauze bandages, along with a sheet-covered, metal-and-wood-platform arrangement.

Shawn did as directed and stepped back. The physician moved in, began his examination, first checking the girl's pulse, then pulling back the closed lids to see her eyes.

"How long ago did this happen?" he asked, turning to the darkened place along her temple and probing gently.

"Not more'n thirty minutes. Was just

outside of town a ways. Some Indians jumped her."

"Indians?"

"Were three of them. Just happened to be close by and was able to drive them off."

Bailey reached into one of the cabinets, obtained a small bottle. "They're getting worse," he muttered. "Been several brushes with them reported lately. Going to have to call in the Army again, I expect."

He bent over the girl, passed the bottle back and forth under her nose. She reacted violently, jerked away.

"Was a hard rap on the head, but nothing serious," the doctor said. "Should be coming to, seems."

Relief moved through Starbuck. "Glad to hear that. . . . Ought to be some rules about a lone woman out in the hills traveling all by herself — especially if you're having Apache trouble."

"There is," Bailey said. "Which way was she going?"

"Southeast — on the road that runs to Phoenix. Was driving like the devil himself was after her."

Bailey nodded slowly, again passed the bottle of restorative close to the girl's nose. She winced. Her eyes fluttered, opened. They were brown, and not blue, as he had

21

supposed, Shawn saw.

"About time you were waking up, young lady!" the physician said sternly. "Was beginning to worry a mite."

She frowned, stared uncomprehendingly at Bailey and then at Starbuck. "What . . ."

"Your buggy turned over, so this fellow tells me. And the Apaches were about to get you."

Remembrance came to the girl. Her lips tightened, and she closed her eyes.

"Good thing he came along," Bailey continued, resuming his inspection of the bruise, "otherwise you'd have woke up in some brave's wickiup."

"I wouldn't have cared," the girl muttered in a lost voice, and then abruptly shifted her attention to Shawn. "Why did you have to be there? Why couldn't you have let me be?"

Startled, Starbuck drew back. Bailey wagged his head. "Now, you don't mean that."

"I do! Anything would be better than —"

The physician quickly laid his fingers upon her lips, stilled the bitter words. "Never mind," he said quietly.

As she turned her face away, he took up a pad of gauze from one of the cases, saturated it with a clear, antiseptic-smelling solution, and placed it on the bruise.

"Hold that right there till I get back," he directed, and as she raised her hand to comply, he nodded to Shawn, pointed at the door.

Starbuck wheeled, stepped into the adjoining room. Bailey, at his heels, pulled the connecting door shut.

"Seems I wasn't doing her any favor."

At Shawn's dry comment, the doctor shrugged. "She's got personal problems, that's all. Doesn't actually feel that way, and I know she's grateful to you for what you did."

"Problems — that's for sure. Any woman who'd start out alone like that for some place —"

"Phoenix, I suspect —"

"Wherever — with things the way you say they are — must have plenty of trouble on her hands."

"It's between her and her husband. She's tried running away from him before, always ends up with him going after her and bringing her back."

"If she's so set on leaving him, it looks like there'd be somebody who'd help her — take her in."

"That's just it — there's nobody, no relatives or anyone she could call a friend, and there are no towns close. . . . Looks like she really intended to do it this time, however, heading out for Phoenix."

"Even if the Apaches hadn't come along, she wouldn't have gone far — not the way she was driving her horse."

Bailey nodded, sighed. "Well, it's nothing for you to bother about. I'll thank you for her, Mr. —"

"Starbuck. She going to be all right?"

"I think so. Bad bruise. Going to be a bit light-headed for a spell, but I don't think there's anything more serious than that. Expect to look her over good before I take her home. . . . You headed for here when you ran onto her?"

Starbuck said, "Yes, came to see my brother. Was told he works in one of the mines."

Bailey scratched at his jaw, frowned. "Don't seem to recall —"

The door behind him opened suddenly. The girl, still holding the compress to her head, moved unsteadily toward him.

"Now, where do you think you're going?" the physician demanded, wheeling.

"Home."

"Not for a while! You're staying right there on that examining table until I'm satisfied there's nothing more than that bump on

24

your head wrong with you," the physician snapped, and taking her by the shoulders, he turned her about and marched her back into the adjoining room.

Shawn stared at the closed door briefly, and then, shrugging, pivoted and walked out onto the porch. Crossing to the buggy, he stepped to the rear, untied the sorrel, and swung onto the saddle. He had done what he could for the girl; she was in good hands now, and whether she appreciated it or not was her business. He had his own affairs to look after.

3

Starbuck cut the gelding about, returned to the street, and rode slowly toward the center of the mining settlement named for the man who made the first rich strike in the area. There were a few persons abroad, some moving indifferently along the walks, others loafing in the shade. At the intersection of what appeared to be the two main streets he paused, taking note of a large mesquite tree to which a man was chained.

He recalled what he'd heard about the efficient if bizarre arrangement: Wickenburg had no jail; instead, simply linked malefactors to the mesquite, where they remained until a judge arrived to hold trial. It was said that no one had ever yet escaped.

He continued on, glance switching from side to side, almost hopefully, on the chance that he would see Ben walking along the street, until he located what looked to be the largest saloon, and there swung into the hitchrack. Coming off the saddle, he looped the sorrel's reins about the crossbar, and turning, stared off toward the bluish mountains to the northwest. The mines would be there, he supposed.

He stood there motionless for some moments, a tall, powerfully built, muscular man with dark, hard-set features that belied his years and reflected the bitter disappointments, the harsh experiences, and the long-reaching loneliness he had weathered during the search for his brother. He was a far cry from the raw farmboy who had begun the quest so long ago; now a cool-minded rider with quiet, pale eyes, he could hold his own among the worst or the best, and in passing left behind a reputation respected by all.

Such was earned honestly and piecemeal, for during those countless months Shawn Starbuck had held many jobs, since the money for the search had to be earned. Old Hiram Starbuck, who had decreed in his last will and testament that Ben first must be found and brought home before the estate could be divided, had neglected to provide any funds for the search; thus it was necessary for Shawn to pause at intervals, find a job for himself, and rebuild his depleted poke.

As a result he had become proficient as stagecoach driver, shotgun messenger, lawman, trail boss, cowhand, and a half-dozen other vocations. Several he found most appealing, and the need to stay put, begin a life of his own, was often strong, but always in the end he pushed the desire aside and rode on; locating Ben was the primary objective of his existence. But he looked forward eagerly to the day when he would finally come face to face with his brother, who had gone storming out of the family fold after a quarrel with their father over a decade ago.

And now, at last, that moment of reunion was close at hand. He would see Ben, and together they would return to Ohio, settle, and share alike the small fortune Hiram Starbuck had accumulated and stowed away in a bank for them. When that was done, he could turn his back on the endless, often hot, often cold trails and find his place in life.

Shifting his gaze, Shawn considered the sign on the front of the building rising before him. "THE MIDAS SALOON." . . . It was a good name for the place, he thought, and crossing to the door, entered. At that morning hour, patronage was light — two men standing at the short bar, three others lounging about a nearby table. The bartender, a slightly built man with a flushed, veined face and black hair slicked down tight on his head, nodded and smiled in friendly fashion as Shawn bellied up to the counter.

"What'll it be, friend?"

"Rye."

The aproned man bobbed, turned to the back counter, where bottles and glasses were ranged on separate shelves. One of the other customers thumped loudly on the planking.

"How about another'n, Rufe?" he called.

The barkeep bobbed again. "Coming soon as I take care of this here stranger."

The two men turned as one, eyes raking Starbuck in the half-suspicious way of local residents sizing up newcomers. Shawn met their glance coolly, waited as Rufe filled a shot glass and placed it before him.

"Be four bits. Rye's higher."

Starbuck laid a silver dollar on the counter, made no move to pick up the change as the bartender hustled off to care for his impatient customer. It was pleasant inside the big room, filled with the friendly smells of tobacco smoke, of liquor, of people. It was always good to be in such a place after days on the trail.

"Been around here long?"

At Starbuck's question, Rufe, back in his original position and beginning to dry a cluster of glasses just dipped in the bucket of water kept handy for that purpose, looked up, grinned.

"Just about ever since there was a town," he replied, pausing to look off through the doorway. "Now, let's see. Old Henry Wickenburg found the Vulture mine in sixty-three, I think it was. I come in sixty-four."

"Tending bar all the time since?"

"Only thing I know how to do, actually," Rufe said frankly. "Oh, I took me a turn hunting for gold, same as everybody else around here did. Picked me up a few nugget and a little dust over on Rich Hill, but was never enough to do any good. Finally decided bartending was what the good Lord intended for me to do, so I went back to doing it."

"Seems I recall some saying about it being smart for a shoemaker to stick to his last. . . ."

Rufe nodded. "About covers it, for certain, and I reckon there's a plenty of folks around here learning just how true that is. What brings you here?"

"Looking for a fellow. Was told he worked at one of the mines."

"Which one? There's more'n a few around, some being worked by partners, some by the owners themselves. And then there's a couple of sort of big ones — corporations. Skull's one of them. Another'n is the Gold Eagle."

"Don't know which it is. Man that gave me the tip was named Jake Wiser. Maybe you know him."

Rufe sucked at his lower lip, wagged his head. "Nope, don't recollect him."

"Plain forgot to ask him which mine. Name he'd be going by is Damon Friend."

Rufe's expression changed. A frown crossed his placid features. The two men down the bar turned slightly, again gave Starbuck close scrutiny.

"You happen to know him? Guess I forgot to mention it, but he's my —"

"Know him!" one of the pair cut in loudly. "Ain't nobody around here that don't know him after what he up and pulled!"

Starbuck motioned to the silent Rufe for a refill, pushed the half-dollar change forward. He was on soft ground, he realized; best to proceed carefully until he knew what it was all about.

"What's that mean?"

"Means he skinned out of here a week or so ago with twenty thousand in gold that

31

belonged to the Skull people — that's what!"

Shawn, the drink halfway to his lips, paused. Ben steal twenty thousand dollars? He'd not believe it. There had to be some mistake.

"Expect we're talking about two different men," he said, and downed his liquor. "One I'm looking for wouldn't ever pull something like that."

"Name was Damon Friend. Was wagon guard for Skull mine. Been in charge of seeing to it that their gold got down here from the crusher to the Wells Fargo office. He the one?"

"Not sure," Shawn said, stalling, trying to collect his thoughts. Could Ben be guilty of such a thing? "How long has this man you're talking about been around?"

"Four, five months."

"Murder charge hanging over him, too," the second man at the counter said. "Killed a fellow while he was doing it."

It couldn't be Ben — he was certain. Robbery, murder — it had to be a mistake.

"You think your friend's the same one?"

Starbuck shook his head. "Doesn't seem likely, but I don't know, of course. Just heard there was a Damon Friend working at a mine near Wickenburg."

The shock and unexpectedness of the charges were wearing off now, and he was again thinking rationally. He'd not mention that there was a relationship, simply let it ride for the time being while he tried to get to the bottom of the accusation, which surely was in error. The people involved would be more inclined to open up, talk freely if they were unaware that he was kin.

"Him, all right, I'd say," the first of the two at the bar said confidently. "Don't never hear a name like that around — leastwise, I never have."

"Me neither," his friend agreed, and looked directly at Starbuck. "He somebody important to you?"

"Just had wanted to see him, maybe have a drink."

Rufe was staring at him closely, Shawn realized, had a puzzled look on his round, pink face. He leaned forward.

"You wouldn't be some relation to him, would you?" he asked in a low voice. "Sort of favor him."

Shawn's shoulders moved slightly. "My name's Starbuck."

The bartender grinned. "Reckon it's just my imagination," he said.

The tall rider scrubbed at the whiskers on his face. "With these I expect I look like a lot of fellows. Going to have to get them off." He raised his attention to the pair at the bar. "You say he was working at a mine called Skull?"

"What I said. Was mightly well thought of up there by Nix and the rest of the men — then he pulled this. . . . Why? You going up there looking for him?"

"Not much use in that if he's gone. Would sort of like to know a little more about it, however, and I reckon the best place for that would be the mine. . . . Could use a job, too," he added as an afterthought. "You know if they've hired on anybody in his place yet?"

"Ain't heard. Think they sort've shut down. That much of a loss hurts even the big boys. Far as the details go, just about anybody in town can give them to you, but if you're dead set on getting it right from the horse's mouth, then go up there and talk to Aaron Nix. He's the superintendent. Be the one you'll have to talk to about the job, too."

Shawn nodded. "How do I get there?"

"Head up along the hills — north about twelve miles or so. Just keep going. You'll come to it."

Rufe said, "Be some other places in between. Little outfits. Skull's pretty big. You won't have no trouble spotting it when you come to it. . . . Care for another shot before you move out?"

"Save it," Starbuck said, touching the men at the bar with his glance. "I'll be back."

4

It was getting on to midday when Starbuck reached the mining camp. As Rufe had said, it was not difficult to locate. There was a fairly large, timber-framed opening in the face of a rocky bluff marking the entrance to the mine, and above it was affixed a sign bearing the single word "SKULL."

Nearby, on the leveled-off area fronting the shaft, was a small house that apparently served as both office and living quarters for the superintendent. Farther over, on the opposite side, there were several shacks and tents which served as housing for the men working the mine. A number of mules and burros dozed in a pole corral a short distance below the flat, and just beyond it, at the foot of a ramp where ore carts were brought to be dumped, were two heavy wheeled wagons. An unpainted water tank set upon a low scaffold, a drip bucket hanging from its spigot, indicated the absence of

a well and furthered the air of imperma-
nence that hung over the place.

As Shawn rode slowly into the center of
the camp, an elderly, white-bearded man
with bowed legs and leathery skin separated
himself from a lean-to off the end of the
corral, and still holding a bit of harness that
he was repairing, came forward.

"Looking for somebody?" he greeted.

Starbuck drew the sorrel to a halt. "For
the boss, Nix. That you?"

The oldster spat, shook his head. "Nope.
I'm Tom Mehaffey. Aaron's down to the
crusher. You in a right smart of a hurry to
see him?"

"Not specially."

"Then climb off your horse and set. He'll
be showing up in another hour or two."

Starbuck dismounted, conscious of Mehaffey's sharp-eyed appraisal. He nodded at
the trough behind the tank. "It all right if I
water my horse?"

The old man grinned, squatted against
the corral bars. "Reckon so, long as you
don't swallow none of it yourself."

"Something wrong with it?"

"Well, that there's Hassayampa water."

Shawn wagged his head, not understanding.

"Tale goes that once a man takes a drink

out of the Hassayampa River, he won't never tell the truth again. And there's them that claim he won't never leave the country again, either."

Starbuck smiled. "Expect I'd best be a little careful then." There was a dull, thumping sound coming from inside the mine. He listened in silence.

" 'Spect you're here about that job," the old man said.

"Was aiming to ask about it," Starbuck replied. "Heard the man who had it got in some kind of trouble."

Mehaffey snorted. "Trouble, hell! Weren't nothing like that. He just up one day and hightailed it with the gold he was supposed to be looking out for. Was better'n twenty thousand dollars' worth of ingots."

The sorrel had satisfied his thirst and no longer sucked at the water in the half-filled trough. Starbuck led him to the corral, hung the reins over the top pole.

"You one of the guards?" he asked.

"Nope, mule skinner. It's me that hauls the ore from here down to the crusher, about ten mile below, on the Hassayampa. Was you to get that outrider job, you'd do your living there, not here."

"I see. Was he the only one looking out for the gold? Seems like a lot for just one man to be responsible for."

"Was by hisself that day. There's two others, usually, that makes the run. Otey Cooper and Dan Linden. Otey does the driving, and Dan's a outrider. This fellow Friend, he was the shotgun man — rode in the wagon with Otey while Dan was scouting ahead.

"This Skull outfit's sort of different from most others around here. Big company owns it — San Francisco jaspers. Wasn't them that turned up first pay dirt, however; was Charley Reeves. He filed the claim, dug out what he wanted, then sold out to the Frisco bunch when they made him a good offer."

"He the one that named it Skull?"

"Yeh. . . . Prospectors are sort of peculiar — maybe even spooky-like. Was a old Injun skull turned up when he was doing his digging. Right under it he found a bunch of nuggets.

"Same with old Henry Wickenburg. Was traipsing along with his pack string, seen a buzzard flying overhead. Hauls out his scattergun and shoots it. Went over to have a look at it where it fell, and right there he spotted a passel of gold. Only natural he called his mine the Vulture."

Shawn agreed, again listened to the

pounding inside the shaft. "Doesn't look like the San Francisco owners have done much improving over a one-man deal."

"They ain't, far as the mine goes. Reckon they figure the vein's going to pinch out pretty soon, and they don't want to get caught with a big investment. About the only thing they've done was change the way the ore's handled. Now, most of the big outfits are hauling their rock to Frisco for crushing and smelting. Takes a lot of time and costs aplenty.

"These here Skull owners come up with the idea of hauling the ore down to the Hassayampa, crushing it right there like plenty others do — only they went a bit further and brought in a blast furnace. They melt out the gold, pour it into ingots. Heard someone say it ain't the purest color a man ever seen, and it has to be run again when it gets to San Francisco, but it sure does make it a lot easier and cheaper to handle."

"This Friend — he was headed for there when he stole the gold?"

"No, for Wickenburg — for town. Skull hauls the ingots to the Wells Fargo people there. They take it the rest of the way."

"I see. Makes it only a short haul. . . . You know Friend pretty well?"

"Only so-so. Nice fellow, I recollect. About

your age, only a little older. Just seen him now and then when I'd make a run to the crusher. . . . Him and the foreman there didn't get along too good, I'm told. Some trouble over Truxton's wife. He's the crusher foreman. . . . Don't think you mentioned your name."

"Shawn Starbuck."

Mehaffey shook hands gravely, said, "You don't look Injun."

"I'm not. My mother did some teaching among the Shawnee tribe. Liked the word, I guess, and shortened it into a name for me when I came along."

"Where you from — in the beginning, I mean?"

"Ohio. Town on the Muskingum River. Folks had a farm there. You always lived in this part of the country?"

Mehaffey swiped at the sweat beading his craggy face. "Colorado was where I was borned. Learned my mule skinning up there, hauling freight for the mines. Only been here since the war. . . . Riding shotgun your reg'lar line of work?"

"Done a few other things, too," Starbuck replied, staring off across the heat-blasted hills.

He had come to a decision; he definitely would not reveal his relationship with Ben

41

— Damon Friend — for the time being. Stumbling onto the very job his brother had held would make it much easier to get to the bottom of the affair, and straighten it out — assuming, of course, he got himself hired.

"Well, you're going to need some mighty fine recommending before Aaron'll put you on. Goes for any other man that shows up looking to work. He's plenty leery now, after what Friend done."

"Got a couple of letters that maybe'll help. One from a sheriff, another from a big politician I worked for in New Mexico as a bodyguard. Few others he can get in touch with if he's of a mind."

"Reckon that'll help some."

Starbuck nodded, clawed at the stubble on his chin. He wished now he'd taken the time while in town to look up the barber, get shaved. A beard was an uncomfortable thing in such heat.

"Was wondering," he said after a few moments' silence, "there any chance this fellow Friend didn't steal that gold? Maybe he got held up — or killed."

Mehaffey shrugged. "Ain't likely. Been a lot of holdups around here, for certain. Road agents and such've been having themselves a real picnic, what with all the gold that's being moved, but I reckon there ain't no doubt he done it."

The old driver paused, glanced toward the entrance to the shaft. A man leading a burro hitched to a dump cart filled with ore moved into the sunlight, angled across the cleared ground for the ramp. A second cart appeared, this one pulled by a mule. Both halted on the overhanging platform, tipped, and dumped their loads into the high-sided wagon below.

Mehaffey eyed them disgustedly. "Ain't working like they ought," he said. "Happens every time Aaron ain't here. . . . Rate they're loading, I sure won't be making no haul today."

Shawn watched the short procession circle lazily, follow out the deep-cut ruts that ran from the shaft to the ramp and back in a tight loop. Men and animals all appeared to be sleepwalking. It seemed a slow, crude way to handle ore, Starbuck thought, but undoubtedly it was inexpensive, and that evidently appealed to the San Francisco owners.

"Two carts all they've got?" he asked.

The old driver wagged his head. "Naw, they got a dozen or more. Bunch is just laying down on the job. . . ."

A rattle of gravel brought his words to a

halt. "Reckon that'll be Aaron," he said, looking toward the far edge of the plateau.

Shawn turned his attention to that point. A man astride a mule was climbing the grade slowly. Mehaffey pulled himself upright, the bit of harness again in his hands.

"The best of luck to you," he said softly, and moved off toward the lean-to.

5

Starbuck got to his feet, took a few steps into the yard, and paused, waiting to see if Nix would halt at his office or go on to the corral. Skull's superintendent chose the former, swinging stiffly on the saddle and simply turning the mule loose, which immediately headed for the water trough.

Shawn continued on across the hardpack and entered the office into which the man had disappeared. A thin, gray individual somewhere in his sixties, Nix glanced up at the sound of the tall rider's boot heels.

"Yeh?" he said sourly.

"Name's Starbuck. Looking for a job riding shotgun. Heard you had an opening."

Nix considered him coldly. "Aim to get in on the easy pickings, that it?" he asked in a sarcastic tone.

Anger stirred through Shawn, but he pressed it back; it was important that he get the job if he was to prove Ben innocent.

"Not sure what you're driving at. . . ."

"The hell you're not! Every saddlebum and outlaw in the territory's heard about what happened. Now they're all wanting to sign on so's they can pull the same stunt."

"I'm no saddlebum, and I'm not an outlaw. I'm a man needing a job," Starbuck said evenly. "There one open here or not?"

Aaron Nix deliberately turned back to the table that served as a desk, resumed his pawing through a sheaf of papers.

"Where'd you hear I needed a man?"

"In town."

"They tell you what it was?"

"Seeing that shipments of gold got to Wells Fargo in town."

"You done that kind of work before?"

"Rode shotgun on a few stagecoaches. Wore a badge now and then, if that counts for anything."

"Maybe it does, maybe it don't," Nix rumbled, and then abruptly wheeled. "I know you from somewhere?"

"Could be. I've been around the country. Can't say as I recall you."

The mining man shrugged. "You look familiar. . . . Well, if you heard I needed a guard, then you know why. Last one I had beat the company out of a small fortune. Makes me plenty careful who I hire on."

"Can understand that. I've got a couple of letters in my saddlebags — references, if it'll help."

"Get 'em," Nix said bluntly, and once more began to search through the papers.

Starbuck crossed to where the sorrel waited, dug into his leather pouches. Returning to the office, he handed the creased papers to Nix, who read them slowly and carefully.

"Sounds all right," he said finally. " 'Course, you could've wrote them yourself or had somebody do it for you. Know anybody in this part of the country who'll vouch for you?"

"Stranger here," Shawn replied, and then, remembering, added, "Got acquainted with a lawman over in a place called Lynchburg. East of here, I think. Name's Huckaby. Pretty sure he'll —"

"Never heard of him, or the town either," Nix broke in.

Starbuck shrugged. He supposed it wasn't absolutely necessary that he go to work for the mining company at the job Ben had held in order to ferret out the facts and get his brother cleared, but it would make it much easier. There appeared to be no satisfying Aaron Nix, however.

"Best thing then is for us both to forget

it," he said coolly, and picking up the letters, turned for the door.

"Now, hold on!" the mine boss said hurriedly. "Don't go climbing up on your high horse. You got to bear in mind that I have to be careful. This robbery wasn't the first we ever had, but it was the biggest — and I don't want it happening again."

Starbuck halted in the doorway. "Could happen again, no matter who you hire. Point is, if it does, it won't be me taking your gold, it'll be somebody I couldn't stop."

Nix permitted himself a smile. "As good a answer as I've ever heard. Question is whether you'd live up to it."

"I would," Shawn snapped, and stepped out into the yard.

Simmering, he crossed to the sorrel, opened the left-hand saddlebag, and replaced the letters. Taking up the reins, he started to mount, hesitated as Nix's voice reached him.

"When're you willing to start?"

Starbuck pivoted slowly. "You sure you're not making a mistake?" he asked dryly.

The mining man lifted his hands, allowed them to fall resignedly. "How the hell can I tell? Figured that Damon Friend was straight, too; turned out I was wrong."

"Far as you know," Shawn murmured.

"Can go to work anytime you say."

"All right, you've got the job. Pay's a hundred a month and keep. I'll give you a note to my foreman at the crusher — John Truxton. You'll be working out of there."

Starbuck retraced his steps to the mine office. Nix had settled onto a chair, was scribbling words on a sheet of brown paper.

"Be a shack there you can move into. Take your meals with the rest of the help. Job calls for you riding with two others — a driver and a guard. Haul is to Wickenburg, about ten miles. Gold will be in one-pound ingots in a locked box."

Starbuck listed without comment, making no mention of the fact that most of what was being told him he'd already learned from Tom Mehaffey.

"Don't sound like much of a trip — ten miles," the superintendent continued, "but it's plenty dangerous. Outlaws make a habit of laying back in the brush and rocks, just waiting for a chance to jump you when you ain't exactly ready."

"With three men, it shouldn't be too hard getting through unless they gang up. . . ."

"What I hope they never do. Reason why I insist Truxton make only small shipments — a couple of thousand dollars' worth at the most. That way there ain't hardly enough in the box to interest a big bunch, only one or two; and if you're on your toes, you can handle them. . . . Truxton was a damn fool to ship out twenty thousand dollars' worth all at one time."

"You think Damon Friend had a gang waiting for him?"

"No, don't believe he did. But if the word gets out that we ship big amounts like that, there'll be plenty of gangs hanging around. That's why I want it known there's only small dabs being hauled." Nix finished the letter he was writing, folded it. "Sure, Friend could have had a gang. He could've been going right along making the little hauls without letting anything happen, and then when he got a big shipment worth the risk, he could've called them in. But I don't think that was the way of it. He just saw a chance to get rich and took it — kept it all himself."

"Where were the other guards while it was going on?"

"Wasn't with him?" the Skull man said in a voice heavy with disgust. "This Friend figured he'd be smart and fool anybody that might've heard about the big shipment. Told Truxton he thought it'd be safer to make the haul alone and in a regular buckboard instead of the hot wagon."

"Hot wagon?"

"What the men call it. The company sent it down from San Francisco for us to use on the hauls. Just a regular wagon, only its all rigged up with boiler plate on the sides and ends so's the driver and guard riding with him will have some protection.

"Anyway, there was one of the crusher hands quitting and was aiming to ride into town with the shipment. Friend told Truxton he'd make it look like he was just giving the fellow a lift into town. Using the buckboard and carrying a passenger, nobody'd ever guess he had twenty thousand in gold under the seat. We know now it was just a way to keep Linden and Cooper from being along."

"What about the man he was giving the ride to?"

"They found him dead off the road not far out of town."

Robbery . . . murder. . . . The first thread of doubt crept into Shawn Starbuck's mind. Could he be wrong in believing his brother incapable of such crimes? Eleven years was a long time, and Ben could have changed; still, there was no positive proof, only an assumption, and he would have to have more than that before he was convinced.

That Ben had started for Wickenburg with

the gold was certain; that he had deemed it wise to go alone, make it appear it was not a regular haul, also was apparent. But from there on it was pure guesswork; no one saw what had then happened. Ben could have been ambushed, killed along with the luckless passenger who was with him, and the gold taken. That Ben's body had not been found could mean it was purposely hidden to further prove he had committed the crimes.

"Give this note to Truxton when you get there," Nix said. "He'll fix you up, tell you what your job is."

"Getting your gold into town — about all it amounts to, isn't it?"

"Right — only don't go trying any fancy ideas. That hot wagon was built to be used, and so far it's worked every time we got jumped. I hear of it being left behind, the man responsible'll be looking for a job."

"You're giving the orders," Starbuck said, thrusting the letter into his shirt. "I'll carry them —"

"Won't be me, it'll be Truxton you listen to. He runs that end of it. Responsible to me, of course, for what he does, same as I'm responsible to the company office in San Francisco."

Shawn signified his understanding, moved

again to the doorway. "How do I find the crusher plant?"

"Straight down the slope, due west. Can't miss it. You heading out now?"

"Might as well get there, make myself known."

Aaron Nix nodded his approval. "Doubt if you'll have a haul for a couple of days yet. Sort of shut down after we took that big loss, but we're digging again now. Already told Truxton I'd try to get a load of ore to him by tomorrow."

Shawn made no comment, stepped into the yard, and strode to the sorrel. Mehaffey, still working on the harness, glanced up as Shawn jerked the leathers free.

"You hired?"

Starbuck went to the saddle, settled himself. "On my way to the crusher plant now," he said, patting the letter inside his shirt. "Got a letter here telling the foreman I'm the new man."

"Glad to hear it," the old driver said. "Just you take a mite of advice from me, and you'll do fine — be plenty careful about getting too friendly with some of the folks down there. . . . So long."

"So long," Shawn answered, and pulling away, slanted across the flat for the trail leading off onto the slope. After a few moments the words Tom Mehaffey had spoken registered on him. He halted, looked back, wondering at their meaning. Mehaffey was nowhere in sight, having moved off beyond the corral.

Touching the gelding with his spurs, Starbuck rode on. Next time he ran into the old mule skinner, he'd ask him what he meant.

6

The road from the mine to the crusher camp on the banks of the Hassayampa River was well-defined, thanks to the wide, iron-tired wheels of the ore wagons, and Starbuck had no difficulty. As the sorrel moved steadily along in the midday heat, his thoughts turned again to his brother.

When it came right down to it, he didn't really know Ben — that was a fact he had to admit. His recollection and knowledge were based on the days when they were young boys, and that was eleven years ago. At the time when Ben had broken with their father, he had been but ten years old, and under such circumstances it was foolish for Shawn to think he could set himself up as a judge of his brother's character.

Yet the belief that Ben was incapable of committing the things he was accused of was firm. Shawn tried to reason it out, analyze that conviction; was it only because

Ben was his brother, his own blood kin, that he was so sure of his innocence? It had to be, for he had nothing else to go on — and that was far too thin to carry any weight with others. Everything pointed to Ben's guilt, and he had nothing concrete to counter that belief — at least, not yet.

Shawn looked ahead. The road, winding broadly down a slope, cut through ledges of rock, red-and-white buttes, and dense patches of brush. There were few trees in the area, only an occasional smoke tree or mesquite, but in the deeper arroyos he could see cottonwoods and what looked to be sycamores.

He should be about there, and since, as Aaron Nix had said, he would have no hauling duties for a few days, he would be afforded good opportunity to look around, ask more questions, and delve deeper into the circumstances surrounding the theft and murder. He would have to use care, however; getting too curious would arouse suspicion and cause others to wonder why he was so interested.

The slope ended, and Starbuck found himself on a narrow flat that extended to the river. The crusher, an arrangement of timbers and wheels, was built into the water, and not far from it on the solid ground he saw the furnace and other equipment.

There were several small houses scattered about one of larger proportions, a corral containing only horses, and a few sheds. Two men were working at something near the furnace, which looked like a huge heating stove; a third slouched in the doorway of what evidently was the foreman's office, watching. Shawn made his way toward that point, drew up.

"You John Truxton, the foreman?" he asked.

The man transferred his attention from the workers to Starbuck. He was tall, in his mid-forties, Shawn guessed, had an irritable, harried way about him. He nodded coldly.

"Got a letter for you from Aaron Nix," Starbuck said, coming off the saddle. "Hired me to take Damon Friend's place."

Truxton's thin mouth tightened. "Never said nothing to me about hiring somebody, and I seen him this morning."

Shawn ignored the man's hostility. "Hadn't signed me on yet. Was waiting for him at the mine," he said, and handed the note to the foreman.

The men near the furnace had ceased their work at whatever repairs they were making, were watching and listening. Elsewhere in the camp two others had emerged from one of the shacks, now lounged against its weathered front, their attention also upon the foreman. The sound of rattling pans was coming from the large building, and somewhere back in the trees at the edge of the cleared ground, a burro brayed.

Truxton finished reading the letter Nix had forwarded. Jamming it into his shirt pocket, he said, "Told Aaron I'd find my own man for the job. Seems he went right ahead on his own."

"Just happened I came along looking for work," Starbuck said, not anxious to get caught in the middle of competing authorities. "If I'd been following the river, I would have applied here first."

"You got references — some experience?"

Shawn shrugged. "Went all through that with Nix. Satisfied him, else he wouldn't have hired me. Willing to go over it again with you, if need be."

John Truxton gave that thought while he studied Shawn coolly. He shook his head. "No, we'll let it go."

"Up to you. . . . Where'll I bunk?"

The foreman waved a hand indifferently toward the shacks. "Pick out which ever one's empty. You can tell by looking if they're not."

"Obliged," Shawn said, and started to turn away. He hoped to be lucky enough to get Ben's quarters, but didn't think it wise to make a specific request. He'd try to figure a way without being obvious.

"Hear you had trouble with the man I'm taking over for," he said, pausing.

"Twenty thousand dollars' worth," Truxton said gruffly.

"Understand there was a man killed, too."

The crusher foreman shook his head. "You seem to know all about it. Why ask me?"

"Happened on your end of the line."

"You some kind of an investigator — a detective, maybe?" Truxton demanded, his lean face hardening. "The company send you down here to spy on me?"

"Not anything like that, and nobody sent me," Shawn replied, smiling. "Was looking for a job, heard there was one open, asked for it, and your superintendent hired me. It's that simple."

"Then why're you asking all the questions?"

"This kind of work calls for a man to bet his life every time he goes out. Just want to know about everything, so I'll understand what I'm up against. Nothing wrong in that, is there?"

Truxton's shoulders stirred slightly. "No, reckon not. Outrider's job's the same here as it is anywhere else. We've got a rig we haul gold ingots to Wickenburg in. There's a driver and a man rides shotgun in it. Outrider stays on his horse, keeps a lookout ahead and behind. . . . All there is to it."

"Unless some road agent starts shooting. . . ."

"They leave us pretty much alone. Rig we got was special-built. Has iron sides that stop bullets."

The hot wagon, Nix had called it. "Makes it good for the two inside it, not much help to the outrider. That what this fellow Friend was — the outrider?"

Starbuck knew the details, but he was probing a different source of information, one closer to Ben than all the others, and he wanted to hear it from all concerned.

"No, was usual for him to be inside the wagon with the driver. Linden was doing the outriding. That's what you'll be doing. New man starts there. Linden will be with the driver — Cooper."

"Makes no difference to me. Was told Friend was alone when he took off with your gold. Why was —"

"Fool idea he had!" Truxton broke in

angrily. "Thought he could sneak the shipment into town without anybody suspecting he was hauling it. Shouldn't have let him talk me into it. . . . Fact is, I got to worrying about it after he pulled out, saddled up, and rode in after him."

Starbuck displayed interest. "Didn't know about that. Was too late, I take it."

The foreman nodded. "Couldn't find any trace of him. Did finally turn up the buckboard he was using. He and the gold were gone."

"Nobody had seen him?"

"Asked around, of course. Couldn't locate anybody who had. He'd managed to sneak into the livery stable where he kept his horse, get him without the hostler noticing."

"He kept his horse in town?"

"Yeh. No stable or anything here at the camp for a good horse, he claimed, so he left his in town. Makes it pretty plain he'd been planning a robbery all along. Just waited until there was enough gold to make it worthwhile."

Shawn felt his convictions weakening gradually. He glanced around the camp, took a closer look — the shacks, outbuildings, a shadeless corral, a shed under which stood a buckboard, the iron hot wagon. That was the extent of it; he had to agree with Ben that there was no place to keep a good horse, and any man who thought much of his mount wouldn't subject it to such conditions.

"Can see why he used a stable in town. I'll be fixing up a lean-to for my sorrel, if it's all right with you."

Truxton's shoulders again moved indifferently. "Suit yourself. Plenty of lumber laying around. Can build it off the shack you pick to live in."

Starbuck sleeved the sweat from his face, flung a glance at the structures. There was one a bit apart from its neighbors; the door stood open, and he could see no indication of anyone inside.

"That one looks good enough," he said, making a guess. "Anybody using it?"

"Empty. Was the one Friend had. Yours if you want it."

Shawn nodded in satisfaction. He'd hit it right. "Good. I'll get busy on that lean-to. Work fine off that back side."

"Reckon you don't mind horse smells, then. . . . That big place, that's the mess hall. Take your meals there with the rest of us. A Mex woman does the cooking. . . . Never asked, but've you got a wife?"

"No."

Truxton gave that consideration, finally said, "Plenty of women in town to be had, so it's just as well. Not much of a place here for a woman — only two in the camp, my wife and the cook. . . . If you missed eating at noon, you'll have to wait now till supper."

"No problem. Had more breakfast than usual, so I'll manage. Sort of wanted to make the ride into Wickenburg after I've cleaned up, get rid of these whiskers."

The camp foreman again fell into a silent study of Shawn. "Go to town — why? Got the idea you was just there this morning."

"No special reason. Like to have a look at the road I'll be riding when we start hauling again."

"You sure that's it? Best you understand right now, I won't put up with no drunks. If that's what you're going after, then don't bother to come back."

"Not it. Just want to look at the country." Shawn was again holding to his temper. He had the job; it would be senseless now to blow it.

"Little hot to go riding," Truxton continued in the same doubtful vein, "but do what you want. Country ain't no different from all the rest around here. . . . Be back in time for supper unless you want to go hungry."

"I'll be here," Starbuck said, and turning to the sorrel, led him across the sun-baked flat to the shack he'd chosen as his quarters.

Tying the gelding to a nearby post, he removed his blanket roll and saddlebags and carried them inside. It was a one-room affair furnished with a double bunk built into one wall, a table attached to another. There were two crudely built chairs, a washstand above which was affixed a broken piece of mirror. In a back corner there was a small stove, another shelf-like table upon which lay a box of matches. The wood box was full, as if cold weather was anticipated. There was little else to show that anyone had occupied the place before.

Tossing his gear on the lower bunk, Shawn dug out his shaving equipment, looked around for a pan in which to get water. He found none, swore softly. He would have to go to the kitchen, see if he could talk the cook into providing one. The length and stiffness of his beard called for plenty of hot water and soap lather.

Putting on his hat, he turned for the door, halted as it opened. A slender figure moved quickly into the room — a woman, young, attractive, with a yellow scarf hiding a bandage wrapped about her head. Starbuck drew back in surprise. It was the girl he had saved from the Apaches.

7

She was dressed differently, wore now a light shirtwaist open at the neck, a pale blue skirt, and gray laced shoes. Her blond hair had been pulled to the top of her head so that a bandage could be more effectively applied, after which she had disguised the white stripping with the scarf. A few small scratches showed redly on one side of her face, but on the whole she looked little the worse for the accident.

"I thought it was you!" She was thoroughly angry, and her widely spaced brown eyes fairly snapped. "He hired you — hired you to keep tabs on me, didn't he!"

Starbuck shook his head. "Don't know what you're talking about."

"The hell you don't!" The harsh words coming from her seemed out of place.

Temper stirred Shawn. "Don't appreciate being called a liar," he said stiffly. "Took on a job here as outrider. Man who signed me up was Aaron Nix. Can't see what it has to do with you."

The girl frowned. "Nix?"

Starbuck said nothing. The girl had to be John Truxton's wife; he'd said there were only two women in the camp, and she certainly wasn't the Mexican cook. Other bits of information were coming back to mind now — the words of Doc Bailey, that she was having trouble with her husband, had several times attempted to leave, that he always stopped her, brought her back.

Shawn swore softly, feelingly. He had enough problems of his own without getting caught in the middle of someone's marital difficulties.

"I take it you're Mrs. Truxton. . . ."

"You know damn well I'm Cassie Truxton!" she snapped. "And if —"

"You're a little mixed up, lady," Starbuck cut in flatly. "Me being here hasn't anything to do with you."

She moved out of the doorway, placed her shoulders against the wall, and studied him narrowly. The ring of iron being hammered into place, as workers labored to repair some bit of broken machinery, hung in the still, hot air like the measured tolling of a distant bell.

"You expect me to believe that?" she

asked. "You want me to think you just happened to be close by when those Apaches —"

"Not particularly interested in what you think," Shawn snapped. "Happens what I've told you is the truth. Be obliged to you now if you'll leave."

Cassie Truxton did not move. "You're taking Damon Friend's job, that it?" There was less hostility in her tone.

He nodded. Abruptly the edges of her lips softened, and she lowered her eyes.

"I . . . I'm sorry. I thought it was just another of John's tricks to keep me here." She paused, raised a hand and touched the side of her head carefully, as if there were still pain. "I never thanked you, Mr. —"

"Starbuck."

She repeated his name, eyes all the while searching his features intently. "You remind me of someone," she added finally.

As well get said and over with, Shawn thought. "Been told I look something like the man I'm replacing — Friend."

Cassie nodded. "Without those whiskers, you would."

"Was getting ready to scrape them off when you came in."

"Go ahead."

He considered her in amused silence,

shrugged. "Couldn't find a pan for water. Have to go see the cook —"

"No need," she cut in, and pulling away from the wall, crossed to the back of the room. Reaching down behind the stove, she unhooked a small utensil from a nail in the wall, handed it to him.

"This was Damon's. He kept it hidden there so others wouldn't be taking it. . . . You'll have to draw water from the pump."

"Seems you know this shack pretty well."

She only moved her head slightly in agreement, resumed her position against the wall. "I'll wait."

"Why?"

"Want to see if you look as much like Damon as I think you will, once you've cut off those whiskers. . . . Don't be bashful — I've seen men shave before."

"Damon Friend for one?"

Cassie's eyes, cool and level, met his frankly. "Him for one."

Shawn moved on by her, and stepping out into the yard, crossed to the pump at the corner of the mess hall. Filling the pan, he started back, glanced toward the men working on the furnace. Truxton no longer stood in the doorway watching them, was now inside his office doing something at his desk. That the foreman had problems where his

69

young wife was concerned was easily understood.

Returning to the shack, he entered. The girl had started a fire in the stove for him. She drew off to one side as he set the pan over the flames to heat.

"Like it better if you'd leave," he said, unbuttoning his shirt. "Not right, your being in here. Your husband wouldn't —"

"Don't let it worry you. I do what I please, and it'll please me to watch you. . . . Where you from, Starbuck?"

Shawn remained quiet for a time; then, shrugging indifferently, he finished removing the shirt and tossed it onto the bunk. "New Mexico was the last place. Been about anywhere west of the Mississippi you could mention, otherwise."

He wouldn't say anything about Ohio or Muskingum; it was evident that she and Ben had become well-acquainted, and he might have told her about his early life; that, coupled to the similarity in appearance she had noted, might lead her to the truth.

The water began to simmer. Dipping up a handful, he moistened his face, and then, taking the cake of soap he carried, scrubbed up a lather, doing it all hastily and with no great care. The sooner he got the job over with, the quicker she would leave, he reasoned.

She watched him wield the razor in silence, and when he had scraped away the stubble and wiped off his face, she eyed him critically, smiled in satisfaction.

"You really do look like him," she said. "Very much."

Shawn, putting away his razor and soap, reached for his shirt. "Starting to think it's going to be a drawback," he said, pulling on the garment.

"Not far as I'm concerned," Cassie said airily, and broke off abruptly as the doorway filled.

Starbuck glanced around. It was John Truxton. Face dark with anger, eyes hard, he stepped into the cabin.

"Figured I'd find you here," he said, stepping up close to Cassie. His voice was tight, barely controlled. "You was told to stay in the house!"

"I don't have to do anything I don't want," she retorted. "Looks like you'd learn that someday. . . . I was about to invite Mr. Starbuck to sit with us at our table in the mess hall."

The foreman shook his head. "The help eats at the big table — not with us."

"Damon sat with us. No reason why Mr.

Starbuck —"

"Plenty of reasons — good ones. And you know what they are. Now, get on back to the house. I'll see you there."

"And I'll see you at supper," Cassie said, eyes on Shawn, and ignoring Truxton, stepped out into the yard.

The mine foreman wheeled to Starbuck. "Want you to get this straight!" he snarled. "You're to have nothing to do with my wife. I don't want you around her or talking to her — anything. That clear? By God, I'm not about to go through the hell I . . ."

Truxton checked the words that were spilling angrily from his lips, looked down. Shawn reached for his hat, set it in place.

"Wasting your time telling me that. Only thing I'm interested in around here is my job."

"Be damn sure you keep it that way!"

Starbuck's mouth tightened. "Said I wasn't interested. You can believe it. Now, let it drop."

"Not about to!" Truxton shot back. "I'll be keeping an eye on you from here on."

Starbuck, moving toward the doorway, pivoted slowly. He was doing his best to stay clear of the Truxtons' family problems, but the foreman seemed determined to drag him into them. Just because there had been something between Cassie and Ben — and likely a few others, from the sound of it — was no reason to believe he would follow in the same path. He understood now what old Tom Mehaffey had meant when he warned him not to get too friendly with certain persons.

"You understand?" Truxton demanded, mistaking Shawn's hesitancy for indecision.

The man's words and attitude were rubbing Starbuck's nerves raw, and it was requiring great effort to remain calm; but the need to hang on to the job as a means for proving Ben's innocence overruled all personal considerations.

"I understand," he said, and stepping on out into the yard, crossed to where the sorrel waited.

8

Standing just within the doorway of the house she and John occupied, Cassie Truxton watched Starbuck mount his horse and strike off down the road that led to Wickenburg. Moments later John followed him into the open. He paused to glance her way, and she stepped forward quickly so that she would be visible to him, all the while deliberately keeping her attention on the departing Starbuck.

From the corner of her eye she could see her husband halted there in the hot sun, staring at her while anger and jealousy had their savage way with him. She half-expected him to break, to surrender to his emotions, come striding over to the shack and initiate one of the violent scenes of accusation and counteraccusation that of late had almost become a daily affair between them. But after a bit he spun on a heel and stalked off toward his office.

She turned back into their poor quarters, badly in need of a general cleaning, and sank into one of the aged rocking chairs. Long ago she had lost interest in trying to keep up the place, make it more pleasant and livable; the heat, the ever-present dust, and the crudeness of the shack itself made that an impossibility.

Someday they would leave it all, move to a fine house in a good town of size and enjoy life; that had been John's promise, made often. But he had predicated the promise on accumulating enough money to make such a move possible, a point that he never seemed to reach. Lord knew he never spent any of what he earned! Other than for necessities, he held tight to every copper he earned. Hell, she hadn't had a new dress in ages — not that there'd be anyplace to wear it if she did.

Married at fifteen to a man almost twenty years her senior, it hadn't taken long to discover she had made a mistake. But a bargain was a bargain; it had been a choice between life in a saloon being pawed over by drunken miners and stray cowhands — or John Truxton.

At the beginning she had tried to be a good wife, but there was no satisfying him and his overwhelming lust, and life soon became one of sheer drudgery from which there was no escape. She found herself virtually a prisoner, and the declaration he made to her after her first attempt to leave him — in which he stated that no matter how often she tried, he'd find her and bring her back — proved only too true.

Men worked together in such things, it seemed. Someone was always watching, always quick to report to him anything she did — or even thought of doing, she believed at times. . . . Everyone but Damon Friend.

He was the first slim ray of hope to enter her life, and during the few months he worked for Skull she had known her first genuine happiness. Toward the last John had begun to suspect there was something between them, and several times in fits of raging jealousy he had accused her of such.

She found it easy to lie to him, and later had taken much satisfaction in knowing that he knew she was lying; this even softened somewhat the blows she occasionally suffered at his hands. But the moments of turbulence, the painful slappings around, the nerve-shattering arguments, were matters of small importance; being with Damon and his quiet, courtly ways made up for everything. . . . He always called her

"Cassandra," never "Cassie" or "Cass," as others she had known would do. Of course, in the presence of outsiders she was "Mrs. Truxton" — something that for some reason always infuriated John.

And then, suddenly, Damon was gone. He made no farewell, simply went on a haul to Wickenburg one day and had not been seen or heard from since. It was like having the sky fall upon her, the world end. The money had simply been too great a temptation for him, she supposed; and then, as she gave it deeper thought, the conviction grew that he had not forsaken her, that she would hear from him again, that very possibly he would send for her.

The belief became so intense that she finally decided to make another attempt to leave — not to wait, but to find him herself. He would be in Tucson, she was sure. He'd mentioned the town several times, had spoken of how pleasant it was there, and that someday he'd like to make it his home. She had started, planning to go first to the nearest settlement, Phoenix, and from there take the stagecoach for the rest of the journey. She had barely gotten underway when the Apaches had spotted her, the accident occurred, and this man Starbuck appeared on the scene.

She still wasn't absolutely certain in her mind that John hadn't hired him to keep an eye on her. It had all been so pat, so convenient, his being there right at the time the Indians had appeared; it was almost as if he had been following her. Starbuck had denied it, of course, claimed that Aaron Nix was the one who had hired him — which could mean nothing. It could have been a put-up job between the three of them.

She had said nothing to John about Starbuck, wasn't sure that she would, for in so doing she would be granting him a certain amount of satisfaction. It was better to simply ignore the whole thing, insist she had fallen off her horse and struck her head, baldly deny any reports to the contrary. . . . A faint smile tugged at Cassie Truxton's full lips. The funny part of it was that, if John had put Starbuck to work watching over her, it was backfiring on him; John was already showing signs of jealousy.

It was strange how much Starbuck resembled Damon, and a little cruel, also. Looking at him heightened the need within her for Damon, reminded her of all he had come to mean to her. . . . There could be no connection between the two, of course. It was pure coincidence. Damon had never mentioned a brother or any other kin, but then, Damon was never one to talk about himself — past, present, or future; he simply lived in the moment at hand.

It occurred to Cassie then that Starbuck could be a lawman of some sort, sent by the mine owners in San Francisco to track down Damon and the gold he had gotten away with. If so, they'd as well forget it. They would never find him; he was much too clever to be caught.

She was glad he'd skipped with the gold. It had meaning for her, she was sure. Damon now had plenty of money, something he knew she had always yearned for, and was probably making plans for their life and future together. Chances were his scheme called for them to wait, lie low until the hullabaloo over the stolen gold died out, and then get together.

Trouble was, she doubted she could hold off that long, especially if it turned out Starbuck was a lawman. He had a sort of grim, patient way to him that told a person he'd not give up easily on anything he undertook to accomplish.

Cassie rose suddenly, crossed to the door, and looked out across the hills toward Wickenburg. Maybe, just maybe, she could turn this Starbuck, whoever and whatever he was, to her advantage. He'd made a great show of his lack of interest when she was in his cabin; but he was a man, and she had yet to meet the one she couldn't bring to terms.

9

The road to Wickenburg followed a course roughly paralleling the river. It wasn't a bad route, Shawn saw, although the brush and occasional masses of rock offered good opportunities for anyone planning ambush. He took special regard of the places where trouble would most likely present itself, if it was to come at all, and made a mental note to pay sharp attention to them when the time came for him to accompany his first haul.

It was around midafternoon when he reached the settlement. He had no exact plan or idea as to what he would do in Wickenburg other than to just nose around and see if he could turn up something that would aid in proving his brother did not commit murder and robbery.

He had put aside, at least temporarily, the possibility that Ben had been killed while trying to protect the shipment of gold in his charge; the fact that his horse and gear were gone seemed to disprove the theory. But he was not abandoning the idea entirely — the missing gear and mount could have been purposely stolen by the party or parties actually committing the crimes in order to throw the blame on him, dead or otherwise.

Reaching the end of the street, Starbuck rode into the hilly town, oblivious of the glances thrown his way, uncertain in mind where to begin. Doc Bailey. . . . The thought came to him abruptly. He had a speaking acquaintance with the physician, and it was generally conceded that a town doctor ordinarily knew his patients well and could furnish much information if he could be induced to talk.

He passed on through the main part of the settlement, came eventually to the quarters of the medical man, and pulled up at the hitchrack in the yard. Motion around at the rear of the house drew his attention as he dismounted, and looking closer, he saw that it was Bailey working in a small vegetable garden, and moved toward him. When he was still a dozen paces away, the doctor heard his approach, straightened, and faced him.

"Got some trouble?"

Starbuck shook his head. "Just like to talk a bit."

Bailey frowned. He considered Shawn for a long moment, turned, and resumed his weeding chore. "About what?"

Starbuck dropped to his heels. "Got myself a job at the Skull mine. . . . Outrider."

The physician paused but did not look around. "Expect you've met Cassie Truxton then — for the second time."

"Seems her husband is my boss."

"So?"

"Just wanted to mention it, and that I was glad you got her home without —"

"Wasn't necessary for me to take her. Went on her own. . . . How come you to take a job? Thought you came here looking for somebody."

"Was. Haven't found him yet." Bailey had apparently forgotten that he'd said it was his brother he was seeking. That was fortunate; he'd let it go at that. "Job was open, and I'm not so flush I couldn't use a little cash. . . . Seems I'm taking over from a man named Damon Friend. Wondering if you knew him."

"When I saw him," Bailey said shortly. "What about it?"

"Reckon I'm just curious. John Truxton sort of jumped on me with both feet after

83

he saw me talking to his wife. Was there a big thing going on between her and this fellow Friend?"

Bailey gave that a thought, glanced on a scatter of chickens vigorously dusting themselves in a nearby pen. "Well, being common knowledge, I don't guess I'd be stepping out of line to answer that," he said. "There was. Pretty serious, too, I expect, leastwise where she was concerned. He wasn't the first, however."

"Sort of guessed that. Truxton looks to be a lot older —"

"About double her age."

"You think there's any chance Truxton could have had something to do with Friend's disappearance — because of what was going on between him and his wife, I mean?"

The physician again stopped working. "If you're asking if John Truxton killed this Friend over her, I don't have any opinion. He could have, and maybe with just cause. And maybe it's just like everybody figures — Friend found himself with a lot of gold on his hands and run off with it."

"Except for one thing. If he and Cassie Truxton were so sold on each other, why didn't he take her with him? From the way I hear it happened, he could have arranged it easy enough. If she could slip off and make a try at getting to Phoenix or wherever she was headed, she could have sure met him somewhere."

"Right — unless it was a spur-of-the-moment idea with him."

"Truxton seems to think it was all planned — his insisting on going alone and using a buckboard instead of that wagon they've got all fixed up."

"Could be," Bailey murmured, and faced Shawn squarely. "What's this all about? You an investigator for the mine owners?"

"No, only trying to get the lay of the land."

"I see. What you're really getting at is, do I think John Truxton is apt to put a bullet in you if you start carrying on with his wife — like you figure he might have done to Damon Friend — that it?"

It was as good a reason for doing the prying as any without coming forward with the actual truth. Shawn grinned, nodded.

"Then I'd say yes. Man's had about all he can take. About reached the point where he can be expected to do something desperate. I'd steer clear of her, if I were you — and have as little to do with him as possible."

"Being my boss, that'll be a bit hard."

"Keep it strictly business and you'll make out," Bailey said. "It's a good job far as that kind of work goes, and like as not you can hold it as long as you want, assuming you're good at it and keep your nose clean."

"What I'll be trying to do, Doc," Starbuck said, rising and turning toward the sorrel. "Obliged to you."

Bailey only nodded, bent again to his chore. Mounting, Shawn doubled back to the street. He had learned very little that he didn't already know or suspect. And where Ben was concerned, it was evident he had only slight acquaintance. . . . What next?

The livery stable where Ben kept his horse. That thought came immediately to him. Undoubtedly the hostler could be of some help if he wished. Shawn glanced ahead, scanned the street. There was a livery barn just to his right. Farther on, past the main part of town, he could see a faded sign indicating another.

He pulled into the nearest, feeling relief from the hot sun at once as he hauled up in the runway of the bulky, shadow-filled building. He waited in the saddle until an elderly man in stained overalls and ragged, dirty undershirt came shuffling from a nearby tackroom and faced him.

"Yeh?"

"Name's Starbuck. Hired on at Skull as outrider. Was told the man who had the job before me stabled his horse here. That right?"

"Reckon it is. Name of Friend. Had hisself a right fine black gelding. Used to come in every time he was in town, saddle up, and take a ride. You aiming to leave your horse here, too?"

"Thinking on it," Shawn replied. "No place at the crusher camp unless I put up a shelter myself, and it's a mite hot for that kind of work. . . . Heard Friend just up and left with a shipment of gold one day."

"That he did. Snuck in here, got the black, and lit out. Weren't nobody seen him do it."

"Wasn't it during daylight?"

"Yeh, it sure was. . . . Can make you a reg'lar monthly rate for looking after your animal — say, eight dollars, feed and currying once in a while."

"Sounds reasonable enough. Friend have only one horse?"

"One was all I ever seen. Why?"

"Oh, nothing much. Was just thinking that twenty thousand dollars in gold ingots would come to a fair amount of weight. Seems like he'd have to have a pack horse."

"Expect he would, was he going far. I'm guessing he had a partner or two waiting somewheres, and they split up the gold. Wouldn't be no big weight was it cut three or four ways."

Shawn gave that thought. "That's for sure. You know anything that makes you think he had partners?"

"No, I don't," the hostler said. "Just doing some guessing. . . . When you aim to start leaving your horse?"

"Got to do a little thinking on it. Rather keep him at the camp where he'll be handy if I decide I don't want to ride one of their horses. Means I'll have to rig up a lean-to or something for him if I do."

"Up to you," the old man said, losing interest. "Been a few of them got their nags shot out from under them on that job."

"Can happen, I know. Worries me some, too. But I'm not so sure about leaving him here, either."

The hostler's head came up. "You meaning he maybe wouldn't be safe here?"

"Not putting you and your place down, but you just said this man Friend came in, got his horse and gear, and rode out without anybody seeing him. Now, somebody needing something to ride real bad could maybe do the same thing. Fact is, I'm wondering if Friend didn't steal himself a pack animal while he was getting his horse."

"The hell he did!" the hostler declared warmly. "Took only his'n. I'd a knowed it if there was another horse gone."

"But he could have if he wanted," Starbuck said, wheeling the gelding about. "I'll do some figuring on what I have to do and let you know. . . . The Midas the best saloon in town?"

"Best and biggest," the old man said, and turned back into the tackroom.

Although there were varying theories as to how Ben carried out the theft of Skull's gold, all were in agreement that he did do it, Shawn thought as he slanted across the street for the saloon. Maybe he was wrong. Maybe Ben had turned outlaw; all things pointed to it, and he was finding it hard to dispute the belief. He had been so sure, so certain that it couldn't be true, that he could find an explanation, but now . . .

Suddenly weary and low in spirit, he drew up at the rack fronting the Midas. He had intended to talk with Rufe, the bartender, question him along the same lines he'd pursued with Bailey and the hostler. But what was the use? His answers would be the same, and when he was finished, he'd be no further along in proving Ben's innocence than he was. Best thing was to just let the matter ride; once he began to actually work for Skull, guarding the shipments, something new might turn up.

For now he'd go in, have himself a couple of drinks, and head back to the crusher camp. It would be suppertime by then. He'd eat, turn in, and get a good night's sleep. Perhaps he'd feel better about it all when morning came.

10

There were a dozen or so patrons in the Midas ranged all along the bar when Shawn entered. They paused, gave him the usual cursory glance, and then resumed their conversations and drinking. Rufe nodded his greeting and moved down the counter to where Starbuck had halted.

"Was rye, I recollect," he said, reaching for a bottle and glass. Pouring a measure, he set it on the bar, added, "You find out what you wanted to know about your friend?"

Shawn downed the whiskey, shrugged. "He's gone. Took twenty thousand dollars of the mine's gold with him. Seems to be about all there is to it."

"Guess you could've saved yourself a trip out there."

"Right, only I did get myself a job. Signed on with Skull — outrider."

The barman's brows lifted in surprise.

"Well, I'm real glad to hear that. Been quite a few around town wanting to hire on." Rufe turned, looked to the men at the bar. "Hey, you boys — like for you to meet somebody. This here's Shawn Starbuck. Nix has hired him to take the job that fellow Friend had."

Shawn was aware of the close attention suddenly focused upon him. Several of those present nodded slightly, turned away. A group of four immediately to his right continued to stare, their features intent, almost sullen. He met their attention coolly — a thick-shouldered redhead; a slightly built blond kid with a rash on his sallow face; a lean, dark man with a pistol tucked under his belt instead of in a holster, as was customary; and a squat drummer in a checked suit that had seen better days.

"I'll be goddamned," the redhead muttered. "Might've known old Aaron'd pull a stunt like this." He took a step closer to Shawn, folded his arms across his chest. "You ever done any outriding?"

Shawn only nodded. In the tight hush that had dropped over the room, Rufe said hurriedly, "Might as well meet these fellows, Starbuck. You'll be seeing them around more'n aplenty. . . . Now, that redhead there's named Turnbull. Most folks call him

Bull. The kid's Billy Jay. Man next to him is Amos Gordon. Used to sell me whiskey until the gold fever got him. One on the end's Cliff Roder."

None of the four offered to shake hands, and Shawn made no effort to push the courtesy. Turnbull leaned back, hooked his elbows on the edge of the bar.

"Where was it you done this here outriding you claim you done?"

The question was uncalled for, could only have come from a man with too many drinks under his belt and looking for trouble. Rufe again bridged the gap.

"Now, that ain't none of our business, Bull. Reckon he satisfied Aaron, or he wouldn't've got the job — and satisfying him is all it takes."

"Maybe," the redhead rumbled. "He just ain't got the looks."

Rufe laughed, trying hard to break the tenseness. "Now, what's an outrider look like mostly?"

"Not like him," Turnbull snapped. "He ain't nothing but a lousy cowpuncher horning in up here where he don't belong. . . . Ain't that right, Mr. Starbuck?"

Shawn was in poor humor for such talk. The fact that he had learned nothing to bolster his belief in Ben's innocence left him at low ebb and bitter mood. Ordinarily he would have considered the source and ignored Bull Turnbull, but not this time.

"You've got a big mouth, Red. About time you closed it," he said quietly.

At once the pasty-faced kid and the one-time whiskey drummer moved a step away from the bar, an eager expectancy in their manner. Roder did not stir, only his eyes showing any change. A tight grin pulled Turnbull's lips back from his teeth.

"You're talking mighty big for a —"

"Hold on, Bull!" Rufe broke in, no longer smiling. "I don't want no trouble in here. . . . Just because Nix hired him instead of you ain't no reason to jump —"

"Only aiming to prove he's putting the wrong man on the job," the redhead said, and began to move slowly toward Shawn.

Elsewhere the remaining patrons had forgotten all their drinks and conversation, were drifting out into the center of the saloon, where visibility was better.

"What do you say, Mr. Cow Nurse?" Turnbull pressed, halting a stride away from Shawn. "You want me proving who's the best man?"

Starbuck tossed off the last of his drink. "Up to you. I'll give you a little advice, however — forget it."

Turnbull glanced around at the onlookers, feigned surprise on his broad features. "You hear that? Forget it, he tells me!"

Billy Jay laughed. "Reckon he'd sure like for you to forget it, Bull."

"I bet he sure would," the redhead agreed, and took another step toward Starbuck. Shoulders hunched, lips drawn back, eyes bright, he wagged his head. "Well, I ain't about to call it off," he said, and lashed out, palm open, at Shawn's face.

Starbuck, frustration, disappointment, and anger surging to the surface in a flashing fragment of time, jerked aside, blocked the swing with his left arm. His balled right fist drove forward, caught Turnbull on the chin, rocked him to his heels. His follow-up left cut a swift arc through the smoky air, cracked solidly against the redhead's jaw.

A yell sounded as Turnbull staggered into the bar, knocking over glasses and bottles. Shawn, temper driving him relentlessly, moved in fast. He caught Turnbull by the shirt front, whirled him about, smashed another shocking blow into the jaw of the dazed man.

The redhead stumbled away, hands hanging loosely at his sides. Starbuck seized him by the arm, again spun him around, hammered two quick blows to the belly. Turnbull's legs quivered. Shawn drove a stinging left to the head, a right to the ear. The husky man's knees buckled. He twisted half about and sprawled full length on the dusty floor.

Face shining wish sweat, breathing raggedly, Starbuck stepped back, sharp eyes now on Bull's three friends. "You want to take it up from here?" he rasped.

Billy Jay made no reply. Roder only stared. Gordon, the drummer, brushed his hat to the back of his head. "His fight, not mine," he said, and looked down at Turnbull. "Ain't no use trying to beat him to death."

Someone in the crowd said, "He asked for it."

"And he sure's hell got it," another voice added.

There was a ripple of laughter. Starbuck eased back to the bar, glance now on Turnbull, stirring uncertainly. His anger was spent, and he felt better. Motioning to Rufe, he said, "I'll take a rye."

The bartender hurriedly set a glass before him, filled it with whiskey. "Was wondering this morning about that belt buckle you're wearing. Can see now that it means you're some kind of a fighter champion."

Shawn shook his head, made no further explanation. The ornate oblong of scrolled silver with the ivory figure of a boxer posed in fighting stance upon it had been Hiram Starbuck's, had come to Shawn at his father's death.

Hiram, a devotee of the scientific art, could have been a champion had he wished, but preferred instead to treat it as a pastime, one he also taught to his two sons. The buckle had been presented to him by admiring friends and neighbors in recognition of his talent.

Bull Turnbull was pulling himself unsteadily to his feet. One eye had swelled, was closing rapidly. Traces of blood showed at the corners of his mouth. He raised his head, stared sullenly at Shawn.

"Wasn't ready," he muttered thickly. "You come at me when I wasn't looking."

"You want to start over?" Starbuck snapped, anger again rising within him.

Bull gave that slow thought. His shoulders stirred finally. "Some other time," he said, and turned to rejoin his friends.

Shawn watched them gather about him; and then, taking up a bottle, all moved off toward a table in the back of the saloon. When they had settled about it, he brought his attention back to the bar, to the remainder of the whiskey in his glass. Several of the others along the counter drifted in closer.

One near the front whistled softly, pointed at the buckle. "That must mean something," he said admiringly. "Way you knocked old Bull around, and him not laying a finger on you. Man have to have some training to do that!"

"For a fact," Rufe agreed. "You sure you ain't one of them boxer champions that goes around the country putting on exhibitions?"

Shawn finished off his drink, dropped a coin onto the bar, grinned. "Like Bull said, I'm just a cowhand," he murmured, and turning, crossed the room and stepped out into the lowering sunlight.

11

The sun, dropping behind the hills to the west, cast a hazy amber glow over the land as Shawn rode into camp. With the clanging of the supper gong in his ears, he pointed the gelding toward the corral where other horses were being kept, noting, as he did, that Cassie Truxton was coming from the house she and the crusher foreman occupied. She returned his glance with a smile and continued on across the hard-packed ground for the mess hall.

Turning the sorrel loose to feed with the company mounts, Shawn slung his tack on the pole rack provided and crossed to the pump, where several men were washing up. Nodding to them, he rinsed the sweat and dust from his face and hands, dried on the well-marked community towel, and followed them into the camp's dining quarters. He was at ease now, the harsh, swirling anger that had possessed him earlier having expended itself.

Cassie and John Truxton were seated at a small table placed apart from the longer fixture used by the crew. Holding his eyes straight ahead, he moved by the couple and found a chair for himself with the men. All glanced at him, a few nodding but making no other overtures.

It was a strange experience to Starbuck, accustomed to the noisy, jocular atmosphere encountered at such times on most ranches. It was almost as if the dozen or so persons in the room were enemies.

The food was good and plentiful, and Shawn, having missed a noon meal, made the most of it. Around midway through the meal, Truxton rose and tapped on the edge of his plate for attention. The men paused, turned to him reluctantly.

"Got a new man going to work. Name's Starbuck. Takes on the outrider job. You can introduce yourselves," the foreman said, and sat down.

The crew resumed their eating as if there had been no interruption. Shawn, glancing along the table, saw no effort being made to acknowledge him, and accordingly continued his meal. A short time later the scrape of chairs behind him indicated the departure of the Truxtons. Not long after that, others began to leave.

The change in their manner was noticeable. They passed by him, one by one — solemn, work-hardened men — and extended their callused hands. Each gave his name and wished him well on the job. Again he was struck by the contrast between them and the usual run of cow-punchers, wondered if the work they did turned them inward, left them with little enthusiasm, or if it had something to do with Truxton.

Two men hung back from the rest, and when all had gone but Starbuck and themselves, they left their places and took chairs opposite him.

"Name's Otey Cooper," one, a tall, lanky man with a full moustache, said, offering his hand. "Reckon we'll be working together, I'm the driver."

Starbuck returned the greeting, glanced at Cooper's partner. The driver jerked a thumb at him, said, "He's Linden — Dan Linden. Was doing the outriding afore Friend took off. He'll be riding shotgun now."

Linden was small, had pale eyes and tight lips. He barely smiled as he took Shawn's fingers into his own.

The two settled back on their chairs. Cooper looked toward the end of the room off which the kitchen lay, waved to a teen-

101

aged Mexican boy.

"Oye, muchacho! Más café, por favor."

The boy grinned broadly, took up a pot of coffee, and hurried forward.

"Bring some cups," Linden said.

The boy paused, returned to the kitchen, reappeared shortly with the necessary containers. Placing them before the two men, he filled both, looked questioningly at Shawn.

"This here's Polocarpio — we call him Polo for short," Cooper said, tousling the boy's thick shock of black hair. "He's a mighty fine little fellow. . . . Wants to know if you need more coffee."

Starbuck smiled, shook his head at the beaming youngster. Three cups of the strong, coal-black brew were enough. Polo turned, trotted back toward the kitchen. Cooper took a sip from his tin cup.

"Can't say as I blame you none," he said to Shawn. "That María — she ain't never going to learn how to make java — not if she lives a hundred years. . . . Truxton tell you we was making a haul tomorrow?"

"Haven't talked to him since this morning."

"Probably leaving it up to me," the older man said. "Being the driver, I reckon that sort of makes me the boss of this here crew."

He paused, looked closely at Shawn, as if waiting for a reaction.

"Suits me," Starbuck said. "What time?"

"Like as not it'll be the middle of the morning, time we're ready. You riding your own horse, or you aim to use one of the company's? Dan here can tell you which ones are fit to ride."

"Use my own unless there's some reason why I can't."

"No reason, 'cepting, if we get jumped, he could get shot out from under you."

It was something to think about, Shawn agreed. He'd mull it over, decide in the morning. In the event of trouble, he preferred to be on a horse he knew well, but on the other hand, he didn't relish the thought of losing the big gelding.

"You been doing this kind of work?" Linden asked.

"Enough to know what it's all about. You expecting trouble?"

"Always are," Cooper said. "Be worse now, since that twenty thousand got took. Word gets about we're going to have a whole army of road agents breathing down our necks."

Nix or Truxton, one had expressed the same fear; Shawn couldn't remember which. "Might be smart to start out with only a little dab — a few hundred dollars' worth — and let them hold us up," he said, smiling. "That way they'd find out we're not hauling big loads anymore."

Cooper laughed, slapped at his knee. "Just might be a good idea at that!"

Linden only nodded. After a moment Shawn said, "You think that Friend stole all that gold himself, or could it have been some gang put a bullet in him and took it away from him?"

"Ain't no doubt he done it," Cooper said flatly, taking another swig of his coffee. "Way he set it up, leaving us here, going alone and all that, is enough proving for me."

"But he could have been bushwhacked, then buried."

"Ain't likely. Whoever'd done that wouldn't bother to plant him. Just wouldn't see the sense in taking the time. Hell, they didn't bury old Jamie — just left him laying there."

Shawn settled back. The answers were always the same, got him nowhere. "You know this Friend pretty well?"

Cooper glanced at Linden, grinned. "Hell, wasn't nobody knew him hardly — 'cepting a certain lady that I ain't about to mention. Was one of these birds that don't never do no talking, just listening. Like a Injun."

"Seems like he wasn't the only close-mouthed one around here," Starbuck said dryly.

Cooper frowned, then smiled. "Oh, you're meaning the rest of the hands. Don't mind them — they don't figure to be unfriendly or nothing like that; it's just that, well, maybe I'd best put it this way: a man taking a job under John Truxton is mighty hard put for a place to work."

"Rough on his men, that it?"

"Plenty. Working on a crusher is bad enough, but when you got a boss whose innards is burning like hell's fire all the time and turning him meaner'n a singed bobcat, then you got yourself some mighty big problems."

"He always been like that, or only since all that gold was stolen?"

Otey Cooper glanced around the room, assured himself they were alone. "Hell, you ain't dumb," he said, leaning forward. "Got yourself a sample this morning. It's his woman. Just let a man even look at her, or her at him, and John starts burning."

"Told me mighty plain and flat out this morning that I wasn't to have anything to do with her."

"If there's ever been a jasper walk through

here he hasn't told it to, I can't remember it — not that it's done much good. That little gal does dang near whatever she pleases — mostly behind his back."

Starbuck toyed with his empty cup. Farther down the table the boy, Polo, was beginning to clear away the dishes, carrying them in small stacks to the kitchen, where the cook was making considerable noise with several pans.

"Somebody said that she and this man Friend were pretty close."

"That's putting it sort of tame. They was a hell of a lot more'n close, wouldn't you say, Dan?"

Linden nodded.

"Truxton know about it?"

"Expect he did, leastwise, some. He had loud words with Friend about something a couple of times. I figure it was over her — but that sort of took care of itself when Friend hightailed it the way he did."

Starbuck gave that some thought, not mentioning his experience with Cassie that morning and her attempt to leave Truxton. . . . Could she have had it in mind to meet Ben somewhere? Was her joining him a part of Ben's so-called plan, or was she simply trying to escape a life she had come to hate?

It was a possibility to bear in mind, look into if the means presented itself. Too, the thought that John Truxton could have something to do with Ben's disappearance was credible now; the two men had had words over the girl, and Truxton in a jealous rage could have laid plans to get Ben out of the picture. . . .

"Reckon we'd best be getting out of here," Cooper said, rising. "Me and Dan and a couple others usually has a game before we turn in. If you feel like a little penny-ante stud, come on over to the shack. You're welcome to set in."

Shawn got to his feet as Linden drew himself upright. "Obliged for the invitation, but I've had me a long day. Maybe tomorrow night."

"Anytime," the old driver said, turning for the door. "Fresh money's always mighty welcome. . . . Seen you moving into Friend's old cabin."

"Was empty and seemed as good as the rest," Shawn said, moving toward the exit with the two men. "There something wrong with it?"

"Not that I know of," Cooper replied, stepping out into the yard. "Could be it's lucky or unlucky, all depending on how a fellow looks at it." The old man winked broadly, then added, "G'night. See you come morning."

Starbuck responded, continued on his way across the cleared ground for his quarters. He wasn't exactly certain what Otey had meant, but he had a hunch it entailed Cassie Truxton. If so, they could change their minds; he had too many other things to think about, because the way it was shaping up, it appeared Ben was either dead or was a murderer and a thief.

12

Shawn got his first close-up look at the hot wagon that next morning after breakfast. As he was leaving the mess shack, Cooper and the man who handled the hostling, blacksmithing, and other similar chores were rolling it out into the open where it could be hitched to a team.

It was an effective arrangement, he had to admit. A light farm wagon had been chosen, since it was equipped with not only heavier wheels but a stronger framework as well, and its overall length trimmed to six feet or so. Four-foot-high shields of half-inch metal were then installed to form a boxlike arrangement with all but the front plate being made a permanent part of the wagon bed.

The forward section was equipped with upper-corner hooks and bottom pegs that made it possible to lift it off and set it aside while the vehicle was being loaded or unloaded. Unlike the three other sides, which had a gun port in each, the front plate was equipped only with a slot through which the reins were passed.

The driver and shotgun rider, upon being attacked, had only to move forward off the seat, crouch, and thus inside the metal box be completely safe from bullets directed their way — except from overhead.

"Somebody laying for you could get up in a tree or maybe on top of a bluff," Shawn pointed out. "Sides wouldn't be any help to you then. Seems you ought to have a roof — a lid."

"One over there in the shed," Cooper replied, "but ain't nobody ever going to use it. Tried it once — was like setting in the middle of a bonfire! I'll bet it clumb up to near a hundred and fifty inside. . . . Bad enough without no top. That's how come we got to calling it the hot wagon."

The other vulnerable point was the horses, which had no protection whatsoever. But, as the old driver explained to Starbuck, even with the team dead, the men forted up inside could hold out almost indefinitely.

"That ever happen?" Shawn asked.

"Once. Was before I was the skinner. 'Paches hit. Killed the horses first off, along with the outrider. The guard and the driver just settled down, each of them watching

110

two sides. Held off them redskins the whole blamed day. Could've gone longer, only when they didn't show up in town like they was supposed to, Wells Fargo got a posse together and rode out to see what'd happened. Injuns skedaddled when they seen them coming.

"But them boys could've lasted longer, had it been needful. We always carry plenty of spare cartridges for the rifles, and a couple of canteens of water. Man can get mighty thirsty setting inside that there boiler. . . ."

Cooper's words trailed off as the rumbling of another wagon drawing near drew his attention. Shawn turned, saw Tom Mehaffey with his four-up of mules swinging into the camp, bringing in a load of ore. The old teamster waved as he rolled by in the big rig on the way to the crusher.

Starbuck swung back to Cooper. "When do you figure to pull out?"

"Going to be later'n I thought. Prob'ly afternoon sometime. Truxton ain't got them ingots poured yet."

Starbuck said, "I'll be ready when you are," and moved off toward his quarters.

Most of the morning still lay ahead of him. As well put the time to good use, he decided, and throw up the shelter he

111

planned for the sorrel. Accordingly he crossed to the pile of lumber Truxton had pointed out, selected what he figured would be necessary, and borrowing tools and nails from the blacksmith, set to work at the task.

It was hot, tiring work, but by midday he had the two uprights, a roof, and one side erected and securely anchored to the shack. He'd let it go at that, not close in the lean-to entirely. It was doubtful the winters were severe enough to require it, but he'd ask around later and get some advice on the matter. If necessary he could always finish up the remaining walls.

Returning the tools to the smithy, Shawn dropped back to the pump and trough. Removing his shirt, he scrubbed off the sweat and dust accumulated during his labors, and then, drying himself with the stained garment, continued on to his quarters. Entering, he pulled up short. Cassie Truxton was waiting for him.

She smiled, giving his muscular, browned torso her admiring attention, and reached for the shirt.

"I'll wash that for you. . . ."

He ignored her, hung the garment on the back of a chair, and dug into his belongings for another.

"Won't need it. Only has to dry," he said.

It angered him to find her there. No good could come of it. "As soon you wouldn't come here."

She watched him pull on the shirt. "Why? Are you scared of my husband?"

"Just don't want trouble," he said bluntly.

"Man living in here before you wasn't scared."

"I'm not him," Shawn said curtly, and stepped back to the doorway.

"No — you only look like him," she countered lightly. Then, "Is there a haul today?"

He nodded, glanced toward the small office building near the crusher. The hot wagon, team in harness, was standing nearby. Hunched in the shadow of the vehicle were Cooper and Dan Linden. Evidently they were about ready to pull out.

Turning his back on the girl, Starbuck crossed to the corral, and cutting out the sorrel, threw his gear into place, aware that Cassie had followed him and was waiting at the gate. The chore completed, he led the gelding past her into the yard and started across the hardpack for the wagon.

"Good luck," he heard her murmur.

The anger in him softened. He glanced over his shoulder. She had moved forward a few steps, was watching him, a small figure in a soft, close-fitting dress. In the driving sunlight her skin had a dusky shine and her hair had more of a golden glint to it. . . . She was having a hard time of it, living in such a place with a man like John Truxton. He supposed he should be more patient with her.

Cooper glanced up as he halted by the wagon, wagged his head. "Not yet. Ought to be just a few more minutes. You eat?"

"Not hungry. Can wait for supper."

"Same here," the driver said. "Heat like this here takes away a man's wanting for grub. . . . Cooler'n it's been, at that, I reckon," he finished, as if an afterthought.

Linden threw aside the cigar butt he was chewing on, pointed his chin at Starbuck's shack. "Seen you putting up a lean-to. That mean you aim to ride your own horse?"

"Figured I'd be better off. I get in trouble, I'd rather be forking the sorrel than be on some animal I don't know."

"Could lose him. . . ."

"Have to take the chance."

"Cooper!"

At Truxton's brusque call from the interior of his office, the old driver got lazily to his feet. "Expect that means we're about ready to go," he said, and turned into the foreman's quarters.

Linden also rose, climbed into the metal-clad wagon, took a place on the lowered seat, rifle across his knees. Shortly Cooper reappeared, carrying a small, hinge-topped chest secured by a padlock. Starbuck stepped to his side, helped lift the box and place it in the vehicle behind the seat. Heat radiating from the iron plates was already making it almost unbearable within the wagon.

"Your job to set the front," Cooper said to Shawn as he climbed in beside Linden. Seated, he pointed to the square sheet of iron propped against a front wheel.

"Them hooks on the top, they fit into the rings at the corners."

Starbuck picked up the panel. It was heavy, burning hot from sitting in the sun. Swearing softly, he lifted it into place, hanging the hooks in their proper loops to complete the square. He glanced at the two men. Their faces were shining with sweat.

"Same as setting in a boiler," Cooper grumbled, pulling the reins through the slot and settling back on the seat. "Let's get going."

Shawn wheeled, swung onto the saddle. As he straightened up, his glance met that of Truxton standing in the entrance to the office. The foreman's jaw was clenched, and there was a sullen glint in his eyes.

Starbuck studied the man for a brief moment, realizing that he likely had noticed him talking to Cassie at the corral, or possibly had seen them come out of his cabin. He shrugged, cut the sorrel about, and spurred to overtake the wagon, now rolling onto the road.

He didn't know what more he could do about the girl. He'd made it plain to her that she wasn't welcome in his shack, that he preferred she stay clear of him. That, and doing what he could to avoid her, left little else to be done.

"You know the road?" Cooper shouted as he drew alongside the rattling wagon.

"Went over it yesterday."

"Good — let's move right along. . . . Got me a feeling about today."

Shawn squinted through the glare at the old driver. "You looking for a holdup?"

"Just what I am. This here's the first haul since Friend took off. Word of that's had plenty of time to spread. Only natural for us to have company waiting for us somewhere along the line."

Starbuck nodded his agreement. "We carrying much?"

"Only a couple of thousand — but they don't know that. They're going to be thinking and planning on twenty thousand. . . . Just keep your eyes peeled."

"What I'll do," Shawn answered, and moved on.

13

Otey Cooper was right — the possibility of a holdup was better than good. Shawn would have to watch doubly sharp. Throwing his glance about and seeing nothing to cause alarm, he looked back. They were moving down a long, gradual slope. Cooper was using the whip, keeping the team at a good pace.

There would be little danger through here, he judged, since it was fairly open country and any hopeful robbers would have to cross a broad stretch of ground to approach the hurrying vehicle. Farther on, where the road cut down through the hills and there were brush thickets and rock ledges hemming the route, was where trouble, if it was to come, would materialize.

He pulled on ahead, widening the distance between himself and the wagon. Best to scout the area well in advance, search for signs of anyone lurking in the undergrowth

— and overhead, also. That was the hot wagon's weakness, and while he sympathized with Cooper and Linden and understood the heat problem, they were voiding its protective capabilities by not using the cover.

Undoubtedly, to fit the metal lid tightly into the sides would create a condition that, in the blistering Arizona sun, no man could withstand. But why not alter the arrangement by mounting the top a foot or so above the sides and thus leave space for air passage? It sounded like a workable solution; he'd mention it to Otey when they got back to camp.

The open country was dropping behind, turning slowly into brushy slopes and washes with occasional outcroppings of white rock. There were few trees large enough for a man to climb and find concealment, but short bluffs were plentiful, and Starbuck, pulling the sorrel down to a slow trot, gave each in its turn close scrutiny.

He saw nothing that aroused suspicion, and pressed on. He could hear the rattling and thudding of the hot wagon and the drum of the horses' hooves back up the road a short distance, guessed that Cooper was still traveling at a good clip.

He gave thought to dropping back, riding

nearer to the vehicle, decided against it. He could be more effective keeping well out in advance and thus being in position to head off trouble before it began. Should an attack come from the rear, he could wheel and return quickly at the first gunshot.

Movement to his right brought Starbuck to sudden alert. At once he swerved off the road, sliced down into the brush. Pistol drawn and ready, he guided the sorrel at a slow walk toward the point where he had seen motion. A moment later he had a glimpse of white and brown working deeper into the thick growth. . . . A spotted horse. Almost at the same instant, he had a fleeting look of a hunched, coppery figure bent low over the pony's neck. An Apache; and where there was one, there likely would be more.

He halted abruptly, listened intently. He could hear nothing except the rumbling of the hot wagon moving toward him on the road. After a time he pressed on, swinging in nearer to where he had seen the brave on his paint pony. Indians ordinarily had little interest in gold, were more attracted by the thought of stealing guns and horses, or simply having it out with the white men involved. A party of young braves was always looking to blood themselves.

He saw no more of the Apache, and aware that the wagon had drawn abreast of him, Shawn doubled back to the road and swung in beside the vehicle.

"Apache!" he yelled above the clamor of the wagon and team. "Headed the other way. Saw only one."

Cooper and Linden, both mopping at the sweat on their faces, nodded in understanding. Linden said, "I'll keep looking," and turned his attention to the far side of the road.

Starbuck roweled the sorrel, pulled out again into the lead. The two men would now be on guard.

The route dipped into a small valley, where the brush again receded, allowing him full view of the slopes on both sides. They crossed, with the wagon no more than a hundred feet behind him, and again entered an area of dense growth. He recalled this part of the country from his passage through that day before, remembered also that this was where he figured a holdup was most likely to occur.

Doubly careful, he searched the slopes bordering the road, paying particular attention now to the overhanging trees, large and thickly leafed here, and to the rims of the shouldering bluffs. But with all his care he never saw the outlaws until they launched their attack. One moment, he was studying the road and its surroundings; the next, four men wearing long, colorless dusters were bearing down on the wagon, two from each side, firing as they came.

They had apparently been waiting in the deep brush at the foot of the slopes, and either had not seen him out in front or else figured it didn't matter. At the first burst of gunshots erupting behind him Starbuck had hauled the sorrel about, and pistol in hand, raced back over the ground he had just covered, the thought flashing through his mind that this was why the Apaches had pulled off; they were aware of the outlaws' presence, were unwilling to engage both them and the hot wagon's guards.

He saw the four riders coverging on the vehicle at the same moment Linden opened up with his rifle. Immediately he snapped two quick shots at the nearest man. The range was too far to be effective, but the crack of his weapon and the spurts of dust brought the outlaws about.

All four halted. Linden began to pour a steady fire at them, levering his weapon rapidly from the depths of the still-moving wagon. Suddenly the riders broke, abandoned their attempt, and made for the brushy hillside.

Starbuck flung two more bullets after them and galloped on to meet the wagon. Cooper, lips pulled back in a tight grin, shook his head.

"Reckon we outfoxed them this time!" he yelled.

Shawn nodded. It would have been better had he been closer and managed to put lead into a couple of them, or if Linden had been a bit more effective with his rifle. As it was, the outlaws were free to try again.

But neither they nor the Apaches made a further attempt during the balance of the journey into town. A short time later, with Starbuck now riding close behind, Cooper wheeled the hot wagon into the settlement and drew to a halt in front of the Wells Fargo office.

While Linden lifted the forward plate off its rings and set it aside, the old driver dragged the chest from under the seat and handed it over to the agency representative, all the time giving a running account of the attempted holdup to the hurriedly growing crowd. Before he had finished, a volunteer posse, headed up by the town constable, was gathering, and preparations to get a search started for the outlaws was under way.

Shawn, slumped in the saddle, took no hand in the proceedings. Hand still resting lightly on the pistol at his side, he continued his job as guard until the gold was duly transferred to the stage company and all his responsibility ended. The posse would find no trace of the outlaws, anyway. Likely they had faded back into the hills, were now safe in some prearranged hideout; they could even be in the town itself, having slipped in unnoticed and unsuspected to take their places on the street.

The Wells Fargo agent reappeared, a slip of paper in his hand. "Here's your receipt, Otey," he said. "Sure glad you made it through."

The old driver bobbed, glanced at Starbuck. "Expect we'll be doing all right from now on," he replied, sticking the slip into a shirt pocket. Brushing at the sweat on his leathery face, he beckoned to Shawn.

"Me and Dan's climbing out of this boiler and going over to Rufe's for a beer and to cool off a mite. Come along."

Shawn had been thinking over the posse's possibilities and revised his ideas some. It would be a good idea to show them where the attempt had taken place. There was still several hours of daylight, and if there was a good tracker in the party, he might pick up their trail.

"Go ahead," he answered. "Think I'll ride with the posse. Be a help if they know where it was those outlaws cut into the hills."

"Up to you," Otey said, and clucked at his team.

Starbuck wheeled. The posse was just pulling out. Spurring the sorrel, he hurried to catch up.

14

The constable's name was Leyman, and during the short ride to where the attempted holdup had occurred, Starbuck became fairly well acquainted with him.

It was a tough job being the only lawman in the area, he'd said, and he was doing the best he could. But he feared the worst; outlaws could now be expected to move in by droves, with every mining company that was shipping gold as their target. It could be he'd have to call on the Army at Prescott for help.

Was he convinced that this fellow Damon Friend had ridden off with all that gold belonging to Skull, or did he think there was a possibility Friend could have been murdered, the body buried, and it made to look as if he'd done it, Shawn had asked.

Leyman had been firm in his reply. "Doubt that. Went and got his horse, for one thing. Belongings, too. Far as I can see, that's proof right there it was him and that he'd had the whole thing worked out ahead of time."

Shawn dropped the subject there, voicing neither agreement nor disagreement, and after they had reached the location on the road where the outlaws had appeared and he had pointed out the direction into which they'd fled to Leyman and his posse members, he continued on for the crusher camp, discouraged and depressed.

He was getting nowhere in his efforts to prove Ben innocent — and from good cause, he was forced to admit. There was every indication of his brother's guilt, and if by some miracle it was possible to prove a denial, there was still the indisputable fact that the gold was gone and Ben was missing, which could only add up to one thing — Ben was dead.

He reached the camp with that thought dully plaguing his mind — either Ben was guilty or he was dead; and this quickly gave rise to a new question: what, then, should he do?

There seemed little point in hanging around Wickenburg and the mine any longer. If Ben was dead and buried, it could take months, even years, to locate the grave, since it undoubtedly was unmarked. Better to look at matters from the positive side, move on, attempt to find some evidence of his still being alive. He might get lucky, find someone who had seen him.

The problem there was that he had no idea of which direction Ben had taken when he rode out, assuming that he did. Prescott lay to the north; Phoenix, and farther on, Tucson, to the south. There was only desert in the west, and to head east meant daring hostile Indian country.

Would a man fleeing the law, burdened with a heavy load that possibly called for the using of a pack horse, attempt either the Apaches or the desert? Perhaps, if he were desperate enough, but it made better sense to think he would choose the less dangerous routes, avoid the larger settlements, and aim for some sanctuary such as Mexico. After all, gold wasn't much good to a dead man.

Ben would have headed south, Shawn concluded after mulling it over. He would follow the Hassayampa River, thus bypassing Phoenix and either going on to Tucson, or if he had been able to lay in sufficient trail supplies, cutting diagonally across the hot sands of the Yuma Desert and reaching the Mexican border somewhere below the prison town.

Deep in thought, Shawn rode slowly across the cleared ground of the camp. The search for his brother had led him to the far ends of the West, but never at any time had he imagined it would take this turn — Ben, a thief, a man on the run with twenty thousand dollars in stolen gold.

"There been some trouble?"

At Truxton's question, Starbuck halted, looked up. The mine foreman, features still reflecting the hostility that had been there earlier, was standing a few feet away. A curious quiet blanketed the camp, and he realized the crusher was not operating; evidently there had been a breakdown.

"A little. Four men jumped us."

"They get the shipment?"

Starbuck shook his head. "No, drove them off. Leyman's down there now with a posse trying to pick up their trail."

"Waste of time," Truxton snapped. "You got the receipt?"

"Cooper does. Ought to be along pretty soon. Stopped over for a few minutes. . . ."

"Always does. You get a look at the outlaws?"

"Too far off when they hit. Time I got in range, they were heading off into the brush. . . . Think you can line up somebody else for this job?"

The mine foreman stared. "You quitting?"

"Like to."

Truxton's manner changed, going from one of sullen hostility and suspicion to relief. "Why?"

"Personal reasons."

"I see. . . . It's all right with me. You willing to stay on till I find somebody else?"

"If it won't take too long."

Truxton smiled tightly. "I'll get somebody quick as I can," he said, and turned away.

Shawn continued on to his shack, dismounted, and led the gelding in under the shelter he had erected. Stripping the gear, he rubbed the horse down with a coarse gunny-sack, and then, using a neckline, took him on to the water trough for a drink. He had intended to build some sort of a manger in the lean-to, but now, his mind made up definitely to ride out, there seemed little object. The sorrel could feed with the other horses in the corral for the brief time they would be there.

Cutting the gelding short at the trough, Shawn brought him back to the shelter and tied him to one of the posts. Later, after he'd cooled, he would get more water and be fed.

"I'm glad you're back safe. . . ."

Starbuck turned at hearing Cassie's voice.

She had come up behind him quietly, but he was not too surprised. He shrugged, nodded.

"Heard about what happened in town yesterday, too."

He looked at her closely. "Yesterday?"

"In the saloon — that man they call Bull."

"How'd you learn about that?"

"Some drummer. Came up from town to see John about supplies. He told us. Told us about the holdup, too, or that somebody tried. Said he heard the shooting, figured that was what was going on."

Truxton had not mentioned he knew about the outlaws and their try at getting the gold, had acted as if he were unaware of it taking place. There seemed little reason for it.

"From what that drummer said, you certainly taught Bull a lesson. I think it sort of made a hero out of you."

Shawn stirred, passed off the comment. "Nothing to be proud of. Lost my temper — and that's always a mistake."

"Cassie!"

John Truxton's words were like a sharp knife. She whirled, startled. Starbuck came about more deliberately.

"I've told you about coming here!" the foreman snapped, anger coloring his features. "Told you plain what I'd do if I caught you around him again!"

The girl had recovered from her surprise. A half-smile pulled at her lips. "You're always telling me something," she said archly. "Do this, don't do that, don't —"

"Get back to the house," Truxton shouted, trembling with rage. "I'll settle with you later."

"There's nothing to settle," Cassie said. "I'll do what I please when I —"

Truxton stepped in close. His arm shot out, and his open palm struck the girl's cheek with a sharp crack. She staggered back, but no cry of pain escaped her. For a long moment she stared at him, eyes burning fiercely, and then, stiff and prim, she marched off toward the house.

Starbuck, his own anger aroused, faced Truxton. "No call for that. She was only —"

"Don't try telling me what she was doing!" the mining man broke in. "I've been through it before — maybe a dozen times! But I'm finished putting up with it. That bastard of a Damon Friend was the last — the end of it! And you, damn you — I'm warning you —"

"Forget it," Shawn said coldly. "I don't need your warning, and I won't listen to your threats. Don't try dragging me into your problems."

"You saying you're not part of them?"

"Got nothing to do with it."

"You're a goddamn liar! I saw her coming out —"

Starbuck's knotted fist caught the crusher foreman full on the mouth, smashing his lips, driving back whatever other words he sought to utter.

Truxton, brushing at the trickle of blood coming from his mouth, fell back a step. The blow seemed to sober him and give him control of himself. Starbuck nodded curtly.

"I'll be gone by dark."

The foreman shook his head. "No need. We can forget this — and you said you'd stay until I found a new man for the job."

Shawn stirred impatiently. "That's going to be up to you. Long as you keep off my back, I'll hang around. Jump me once more about your wife, and I'll pull out. Clear?"

Truxton was silent for a long, hate-filled breath; then, ducking his head, he muttered, "Clear," pivoted on a heel, and struck off across the yard for his office.

Starbuck's impatience to move on mounted. Ore piled up while the crusher remained inoperative; Truxton, involved in repairing the machinery, had found no time to look for a replacement, and though Otey Cooper had pleaded for Shawn to stay on the job — at least until the next haul into Wickenburg had been made. A week dragged by, and then all was back to normal again, with the crusher pulverizing the chunks of rock fed into it, the blast furnace roaring day and night as it did its job.

"Going to be a big haul again," Cooper said glumly that morning as Starbuck helped him roll out the hot wagon and hitch up the team. "Truxton said we'd be carrying pretty close to ten thousand."

"Thought they'd made up their minds to send the gold down only in small amounts."

"That's what they want to do, only this holdup on account of the crusher busting a gut's shorted them highfalutin' owners in Frisco, and they're hollering for gold. Nix told Truxton to go ahead, make the shipment, only be sure we used the wagon. . . . You seen Dan?"

"Not since breakfast," Shawn replied. "Heard him say something about taking a ride, that he was tired of laying around here waiting."

"Does that once in a while. Always was a great fellow for riding. . . . Expect he'll be along before time to pull out. . . . Truxton said anything to you about finding a man to take your job?"

"Not yet."

"Heard him talking about it to Nix. Reckon they're both looking." The old driver paused, scratched at his jaw. "Well, I ain't wishing you no bad luck, but I'm hoping it'll be a spell yet."

Starbuck said nothing, began to connect the harness traces to the single tree on his side. Cooper, following a like procedure on the opposite flank, again hesitated, shifted the cud of tobacco stored in one cheek, and spat.

"John climb you anymore about his woman?"

"No."

"Well, you hadn't ought to feel too hard at him about it. Just his way."

"Maybe so. Got a little mad, however, especially when there was no reason for it."

"Hell, he sees a reason in every man that walks by, being a mighty jealous sort. Was pure hell around here when that Friend was working the job. They was real careful about it, though, never done no meeting out in the open like he's seen you and her do. But old John was suspecting it all the time. Reckon you could say he knew what was going on, same as we all did, only he never could catch them at it."

"Guess it was pretty serious."

"For her, I'd say so. Ain't sure about Friend. Struck me as a fellow that took things as they come, never let nothing get too big and important. . . ."

"He let twenty thousand dollars' worth of gold get important enough to turn him into an outlaw!" Starbuck said bitterly — and without thought.

He looked away, feeling Otey Cooper's wise, old eyes searching him closely. After a moment the teamster spat again, resumed his work with the harness.

"Yeh, reckon he did," he said. "But a man's liable to lose his head and do plenty of fool things over that much gold. Got to keep remembering, he's only a human like everybody else."

Shawn smiled faintly in relief. His unseemly burst of words had undoubtedly reflected more than casual interest in Damon Friend, but Cooper had chosen to let them pass unquestioned, either deeming such questions unnecessary or judging the matter to be none of his business.

"Be hard to live with yourself, I'd think, if you'd stolen that much gold. You'd remember every time you went to use it how you got it. . . . Where'd you think he'd go to hide after pulling a stunt like that?"

Otey answered readily. "Why, was it me, I'd light out for Mexico fast as I could go. Be the closest, safest place. . . . There comes Dan now. He can help me finish up the hitching. You best get your horse. We'll be pulling out in thirty or forty minutes."

15

They left the crusher camp an hour or so short of noon. Starbuck, some of Cooper's misgivings at the amount of gold they were transporting rubbing off on him, rode close to the wagon; and then, when they finally were out of the open country and dropping down into the brushy hills, he moved out ahead as before.

Now, taut, left hand riding the butt of the heavy forty-five on his hip, eyes switching from side to side, he raked the slopes and narrow washes and low buttes ceaselessly in a probing search. He saw nothing that aroused suspicion, but it was not in him to relax his vigilance in the slightest.

The miles slid steadily by, filled with the rumble of the wagon, the thudding of the horses' hooves, an occasional shout from Otey Cooper as he urged his team up a steep grade or across a sandy arroyo. The growth along the shoulders of the road thickened, the taller trees came into sight. They were approaching the area where he had spotted the Apache and the holdup had been attempted by the four outlaws a week or so ago. He should be ranging farther ahead.

Half-turning, Shawn signaled to Cooper and Linden, made it clear he was lengthening his patrol. The old driver waved back, signifying his understanding. There was no response from Dan Linden, the guard leaving it all up to Cooper as was customary. . . . If they ran into trouble again, he hoped Linden would do better with his rifle than before.

Even at such close range for a long gun, he had been unable to hit any of the road agents. Cooper had joshed the man about it later at the supper table, but Linden had explained it, saying he feared hitting Shawn, on down the road beyond the outlaws.

Starbuck guessed that was it; the quartet had been more or less trapped between him and the wagon, and a bullet fired by Linden could have struck him. But there had been those succeeding moments when the outlaws were making a run for the hills, and it seemed to Shawn that the guard could have made effective use of his weapon then if only he had thought to do so. Such just hadn't occurred to him, he'd told Cooper.

Shawn glanced to his right. It was in that area he'd seen the brave on his spotted pony. All appeared quiet and devoid of life. He glanced over his shoulder. The hot wagon was not in sight, lost to view around a wooded bend in the road, but the sound of its coming was a continuing thunder on the hot, still air.

Abruptly a rider spurted into view a quarter-mile farther down the way. Starbuck instantly spurred ahead, eyes on the man, now racing away. It could be an attempt to draw him off, he realized, and slowed the sorrel to a trot. Best to play it safe, not put too much distance between himself and the wagon.

A half-mile on the rider rounded a curve, vanished. Shawn, cautious, continued on at ordinary pace, watchful and determined not to get sucked into a trap. He reached the bend, halted. The man, whoever he was, was not to be seen. Starbuck, puzzled, allowed the sorrel to move on at a slow walk. Was the rider simply a pilgrim traveling the same road, and aware that the area was considered a favored haunt of outlaws, had he become frightened and hurried on when he saw another horseman approaching? Or was he a part of some plan?

Shawn brushed at the sweat on his face, considered the advisability of dropping back to the wagon, telling Otey and the shotgun guard of the incident, thus putting them on alert. Under the circumstances it might not be wise; it could be best to stay well ahead and thereby be able to give them warning well beforehand.

He swiped again at his eyes as he considered the choice. Off to his right, a squirrel chattered noisily in an oak tree, and overhead a flock of crows was stringing raggedly toward the settlement. Elsewhere there was silence, broken only by the buzzing and clacking of insects in the brush.

Silence!

It came to him like a flash of lightning; he could not hear the hot wagon! The rattling, clanking vehicle should be drawing nearer, and therefore more audible. There was no sound at all!

Roweling the sorrel, Starbuck wheeled, sent the big gelding galloping back up the road. Something or someone had caused Cooper to halt. A holdup was unlikely. No shots had been fired. He reached the sharp bend, veered in close to the brush and trees, and, pistol in hand, made the turn. Fifty yards farther on he saw the hot wagon off on the shoulder, horses grazing indifferently

141

on the thin grass. He could see neither Cooper nor Linden.

Cautious, he kept the sorrel at the edge of the thick growth bordering the road, hauled him down to a walk. There was no reason for the old teamster to pull up, and aware of the dangers along the way, he would not have done so unless forced by an emergency. But what kind of an emergency? And where were the two men?

A dozen paces short of the vehicle, Starbuck halted, swung off the saddle. Hanging the reins over a clump of oak brush, gun still leveled, he worked his way quietly toward the wagon, standing hot and silent in the streaming sunshine.

He froze. A slumped form lay half on, half off the seat. Cooper, he thought, but he wasn't sure. Tense, he resumed his careful approach. Where was Linden? Was he lying full length in the wagon's bed? Why had there been no shots fired — either by the attackers, if there had been an attack, or by the guard while the assault was being made?

Starbuck reached the quiet horses, halted. Glancing about, he could see nothing, and after a moment, still crouched low, he moved to the front of the wagon, craned to see over the forward plate. A gusty sigh slipped through his lips. It was Otey Cooper.

A smear of crusted-looking blood plastered his back where a knife had been plunged into his body. Death had come suddenly to the old teamster.

Grim, Shawn drew in closer. Avoiding the heated metal sides of the wagon, he looked inside, frowned. Linden was not there. He had expected to see the guard sprawled on the floor either wounded or dead, as was Cooper. There was nothing to be seen except the canteens of water; the chest of Skull gold was gone.

Starbuck pulled back. It could mean only one thing: there had been a holdup, and Linden was in on it. Following some pre-arranged plan, the guard and whoever else had joined him in the scheme had waited for the right moment, struck, killed Otey Cooper, and taken the gold. Shawn swore deeply; they had chosen the time when he was far out ahead and the hot wagon was hidden from him by a bend in the road. Only Linden could have devised such a plan — complete even to the decoy rider who had sought to lead him even farther away.

But the outlaw party would have been on horses, and horses leave tracks. He had that much to go on. Taut, Shawn circled the team, began to examine the ground on the opposite side of the wagon. There were any number of hoofprints in the loose dust, but more of a concentration at the rear of the vehicle. Three or perhaps four horses, he guessed. They had come up on the wagon from the back, blind side, had remained there, probably while Linden used his knife on Cooper. After that he would have handed the chest of ingots to them.

Shawn lifted his glance, swept the farther shoulder of the road with narrowed eyes, searching for the tracks that would indicate the direction Linden and the outlaws had taken. A dozen steps away he spotted them — hoofprints of two horses walking side by side into the brush. The marks of two others were nearby.

They were heading into the higher hills. It shouldn't be too difficult to follow them if he set out to do so immediately. He gave that some thought, weighed the wisdom of riding on into Wickenburg, summoning Constable Leyman and a posse, ruled it out. It would take too long; the outlaws could easily get beyond reach before a pursuit could be organized. Too, a dozen men riding through the brush would quickly be heard and spotted, and thereby easily avoided. One man alone, moving quietly and while the trail was fresh and the outlaws still near, could be far more effective.

Coming about, Shawn started across to the waiting sorrel, paused, glance on Cooper. He had no choice but to leave the driver where he lay, hope some passing traveler would take note of the stalled wagon, investigate, and then drive the vehicle on into Wickenburg or back to the crusher camp.

He continued on. A sudden splatter of rifle shots broke the hush. He jerked away, hunched close to the side of the hot wagon. He'd been wrong — the outlaws had not ridden off into the hills, instead had waited for him to return, step into the open. Now they were going to kill him too, thus leaving no one to tell of the murder and robbery.

Bullets were spanging into the metal sides of the wagon, screaming into space. Others thudded into the wood parts; more were kicking up geysers of dust around his feet. He was helpless to fight, and he'd never make it to the shelter of the brush. They had him cold, pinned down, and it would be only a matter of moments until one of their shots drove into him.

A bullet whipped through the slack in his shirt sleeve. He flinched, pulled aside. Abruptly his hat was swept from his head, sailed off toward the road. It was a moment made for him. He threw up his arms as if struck, staggered against a nearby rear wheel, spun, and fell to the ground. Immediately the shooting ceased.

Sprawled in the dust, he waited. If luck was with him, the outlaws would not bother to look close, would consider him dead, and move on. . . . If not — well, his gun was still in his hand. He'd get a couple of them before they managed to finish him off.

16

Motionless on the hot ground, Starbuck waited out the long, tedious moments. He could hear no sound other than the clicking of insects in the brush, the munching of the horses as they cropped the dry grass.

He delayed a full five minutes or longer, then cautiously raised his head. The shots had come from somewhere higher up on the slope to his left. Straining, he sought to locate some indication of the men — a bit of motion, a flash of color.

There was nothing. Evidently they had figured him for dead and ridden on. But he was not absolutely certain, and stalling another few minutes while he got himself ready, Starbuck rolled suddenly to one side, bounded to his feet, and lunged for the thick brush a dozen strides away.

No bullets challenged his actions, and finally accepting the belief the outlaws were gone, he returned to the wagon.

The thought of leaving the body of Otey Cooper there in the hot sun still didn't set with him, and stepping up to the team, he turned the wagon around. Pulling the reins through the slot in the front iron plate and securing them so they would not become slack and fall, he started the horses back up the road for the crusher camp. Once under way, they would continue on until they reached familiar surroundings.

He stood for a few moments, eyes on the rig now disappearing in a rolling cloud of dust. It occurred to him then that the outlaws, if they were anywhere within hearing distance, would become aware of the hot wagon's passage. They would wonder at that, likely assume the team had made the move of their own accord. Whatever, it didn't matter.

Checking his pistol, Shawn returned to the sorrel, and taking up the leathers, walked to the point on the shoulder of the road where he had located the hoofprints of the outlaws' horses. They led onto a narrow path, a game trail used by deer and other animals. It angled up the slope in a southerly direction.

Going onto the saddle, Starbuck headed up the grade, letting the gelding pick his way, since there was no indication of any turnoffs. The trail continued for a good hundred yards, doubled back onto a fairly wide ledge. The bright glint of brass near the center of the rocky shelf caught his eye. Halting, he leaned far over on the saddle and picked up one of the dozen or so casings that were scattered about. Spent rifle cartridges. This was where the outlaws had waited for him to return to the wagon, and then opened fire.

He looked to the opposite end of the ledge. Sharp-cut impressions and disturbed shale proved they had continued on the same course after being convinced they had killed him. That was good, he thought as he put the sorrel into motion again; there was a better than good chance they would not have heard the team and wagon as it headed back for the camp, since they had taken a course that led them deeper into the hills and directly away from the road.

There were five in the party now. Evidently the man he had seen and who had endeavored to draw him even farther away from the wagon prior to the holdup had rejoined his friends. . . . Or there could be six, all told. It was difficult to tell without dismounting and examining the prints closely. It was a matter of small importance, anyway, not worth the time it would require to be exact. Overtaking them was what counted.

He understood the reason now why Dan Linden had failed so completely to score with his rifle during that first encounter with the gang. Undoubtedly they were the same men who had taken part in this murder and theft. It was likely that the previous attempt had been a mistake; they had somehow gotten their signals mixed and moved in on the hot wagon when it was carrying only a small amount of gold.

And those rides Linden took into the hills at various times — Shawn was certain now they weren't for the sheer pleasure of being in the saddle, as the guard claimed. They were the means by which he kept in contact with his outlaw friends and was able to have them waiting in ambush at the proper place and time.

Starbuck raised his eyes. The trail continued to climb, working its way steadily toward a ridge a quarter-mile or so in the distance. Beyond it reared higher mountains, green with growth and striped with white where ledges of rock thrust forth from the surface. Somewhere in the endless rolls and valleys the outlaws would have their hideout — an old abandoned prospector's shack, a worked-out mine shaft, or perhaps there was even a small town where they figured they could lie low in safety for a time.

He gained the ridge, halted. The sorrel was blowing hard from the climb. Swinging down, Shawn moved to the opposite side of the flinty little meadow capping the divide, threw his glance down into the valley below. The oak brush and other growth were dense and quickly swallowed the trail. It was impossible to tell if there were any travelers following it from that point; he could only continue to be guided by the tracks left by the horses.

Turning, he started back to the sorrel, stopped. The battered and split remains of the wooden box the gold had been shipped in lay partway down the slope. When the outlaws had paused to breathe their horses after the hard climb, they had utilized those minutes to break open the chest. Likely they had distributed the ingots among themselves, storing them in their respective saddlebags so that the burden on one horse would not be so great.

Moving on, Starbuck again mounted and resumed the pursuit. It was now much easier on the gelding, since they were dropping off the ridge into the valley on a gentle grade. Time wore on. The heat in the deep swale was intense, and there was little shade of consequence available, even if he dared waste any time within it. Rocks mirrored the sun's relentless blast, and toward the end of the afternoon Starbuck found himself riding with hat tipped low over his face as he sought to ease the burning and smarting in his eyes.

They had reached the floor of the valley, crossed an expanse divided by a dry creek bed, and begun the ascent of the opposite slope. The sorrel was beginning to show signs of wear. The continual travel with only a few brief pauses and the blistering temperature were combining to break down the big gelding. He should halt, Shawn knew, allow the horse to rest for a decent interval, but night was now not too far off, and unless he caught up with the killers or at least got them located before darkness fell, he could lose them.

He pressed on, more slowly now. . . . By that hour the team and the hot wagon, with Otey Cooper's dead body inside, would have reached the crusher camp, either on their own or by the aid of someone encountering the rig on the road. Speculation as to what had happened would be running wild, and since he was a stranger in their midst, he could be sure there'd be those who would believe that he, like Damon Friend, had fled with gold after murdering Cooper and Linden, whose body had yet to be found.

It would be a normal assumption, and he supposed he shouldn't blame them; they knew Cooper and Dan Linden well, scarcely could call him by name. And they would recall that he had taken much interest in Damon Friend and in the manner in which he had staged his robbery. Such would be considered ample proof. In addition, there . . .

Shawn drew to a quick stop. Ahead, not far, a horse had stamped wearily. Instantly he swung off the trail, dismounted, and tying the sorrel to a clump of cedar, began to make his way quietly toward the sound. The path was climbing gently at this point, about halfway up the hillside, and he had little difficulty.

A moment later he dropped to a crouch. A small clearing lay before him. In the center was a sagging, weathered shack; on beyond, a dark hole in the face of a butte, framed by rotting timbers, marked the entrance to a mine shaft. Nearby, in a makeshift corral, were several horses.

Starbuck settled back in satisfaction. Subconsciously touching the butt of his pistol to reassure himself of its presence, he studied the clearing and the shack, getting the arrangement firmly fixed in his mind. He could hear a mutter of voices coming from the dilapidated structure, guessed the outlaws were all inside.

Careful, he moved on through the brush, staying parallel and just within the fringe of the growth encircling the open ground. When he reached a point directly opposite the rear of the cabin, he rose, swiftly crossed over. Pressed against the rough log wall, he could hear the men plainly now — plans to spend the night there and then ride out in the morning for some, others to simply lie low and wait for the chance to rob another gold shipment.

Starbuck's jaw set in a grim angle. The outlaws had a surprise coming — they were going nowhere except back to Wickenburg with him, where they would face charges of murder and robbery. Quietly he moved forward along the side of the shack, pointing for a small window near the front. There would be five or possibly six men in the gang; it would be smart to have a look, know just what he would be facing when he stepped through the doorway.

He reached the window, crouched below it. Removing his hat, Shawn started to rise, stiffened as he felt the round, hard muzzle of a pistol press against his spine.

"You looking for somebody special?" a vaguely familiar voice asked.

17

Raising his hands slowly, Starbuck silently cursed himself for his carelessness. He had just taken it for granted that all of the outlaws were inside the cabin. That brief lapse of caution could now cost him his life, he realized.

He felt a lightness on his hip as the man behind him lifted his forty-five from its holster, heard a rustling sound as the outlaw stepped back.

"Get moving. Door's around front." The words were sharp, clipped.

Shawn obeyed silently, desperately seeking an opportunity to somehow trick the outlaw, escape the pistol pressing into his backbone before the others inside the shack became aware of his capture. But there was little hope. It was no more than a dozen paces to the entrance, and the muzzle of the weapon digging into him gave no quarter.

He reached the open doorway, paused, eyes sweeping over the four men lounged against a back wall. Surprise rocked him. Besides Linden there was Bull Turnbull, the pasty-faced Billy Jay, and the gunman called Cliff Roder. He turned his head slightly for a glimpse of the man holding a gun on him, knew before his glance touched the sleazy checked suit that it would be Gordon, the former whiskey drummer.

"What the hell?" Linden exclaimed, his jaw sagging. "You was laying dead . . ."

Their surprise was equal to his. Shawn gave them a hard smile, shook his head.

"You just figured he was," Gordon said dryly, and jabbed sharply. "Get inside."

Starbuck stepped into the shadowy room. There was a lantern hanging from a hook in the low ceiling, but no one had troubled to light it. A pile of gray, faded dusters, like those worn by the outlaws who had attempted to stop the hot wagon several days earlier, lay on a nail keg beneath the window. . . . It was as he had thought it would be; Linden was a part of a gang. What did come as a shock was who the other members were, and that Gordon, seemingly the luckless, down-at-the-heels whiskey drummer, was apparently the leader.

Turnbull was now grinning broadly.

"Where'd you catch him, Amos?"

The drummer, standing close behind Shawn, reached out, gave the tall rider a hard shove, sent him stumbling into a far corner.

"Set there quiet," he said. "Try something and I'll cut your throat. . . . Caught him looking in the window."

"Must've trailed us here," Linden murmured. "Sure thought he was dead."

"Same as is anyway," Billy Jay observed. "Can't let him go running loose. Have to get rid of him."

"Job I'm claiming," Bull Turnbull said, and started to rise.

"Not around here," Gordon cut in. He had a cold, ruthless face, looked totally unlike the man Starbuck had met in Rufe's saloon. "We got it too good to do something that might start the soldiers poking around here."

"Soldiers? What soldiers?" It was Roder.

Gordon swore impatiently. "Goddamnit, Cliff, don't you ever pay attention to nothing? Didn't you hear Dan telling how the mine owners've decided to send to Prescott for the Army, see if they can't stop the holdups that's going on?"

The gunman wagged his head, shrugged. "Reckon I wasn't around. . . ."

"The hell you wasn't!" Gordon snapped. "You and Billy Jay was setting right alongside of Bull when he was saying it. Trouble is, you don't ever listen, and you don't even use your head. You're dumb, thick-skulled . . ."

Roder's features had darkened. He drew up stiffly. "Back off, mister. You maybe're running this outfit, but I don't take that kind of talk off'n nobody!"

Gordon's lips curled. "Do tell!" he said sardonically. "I'm shaking all over." Abruptly he leaned forward, looked directly at the gunman. He still had Starbuck's pistol in one hand, his own, a short-barreled, bulldog revolver, in the other.

"Mister, in the part of New York City where I grew up, we called your kind Sunday-school-goers. I could walk up to just about any man on my street, and for a handful of coppers get you killed and thrown in the river — so don't go trying that tough gunslinger lingo on me!"

A complete silence had fallen upon the outlaws. It continued for several moments after the whiskey drummer had finished speaking, and then Roder, forcing a grin, wagged his head.

"Hell, Amos, I wasn't meaning —"

"Just what I'm talking about," Gordon

159

broke in savagely. "You never mean nothing — you never think. I ain't so sure I want you around. Best thing you can do is take your share of the gold and pull out."

Roder looked at the stacks of ingots ranged before the men on a ragged piece of blanket spread out on the floor.

"If you do, you're to get clean out of the country. Understand? Don't want you even in the territory. With no more brains than you've got, you're apt to spill all you know — and I've worked too damned hard setting up this deal to have it spoiled."

"I ain't going," Roder said woodenly.

Gordon stared at the man, a baffled look on his face, finally drew back. "All right, but by God, you'd best be changing your ways. I ain't got the time to be worrying about you."

"Be no need," the gunman replied in a low voice.

The tenseness was broken. Billy Jay laughed, jerked a thumb at Starbuck. "We was talking about him. If you don't aim to kill him . . ."

"Never said that," the drummer answered wearily, tossing Shawn's pistol onto the pile of dusters and thrusting his own into the side pocket of his pants. "Said we'd not do it around here. Come morning, a couple of you'll take him up to that old mine . . ."

"The Holloway place," Linden completed.

"The Halloway place, throw him down the shaft with them others. Won't never be found there, so there won't never be nothing said."

Bull Turnbull rubbed his big palms together, grinned widely at Starbuck. "Still claiming that little job for myself. Like I said, me and that bucko've got some going around to do."

"Nope, not you," Gordon said flatly. "You're too anxious — and being anxious can cause mistakes. All I want is him taken up there, a bullet put in his head, and the body dropped into that shaft."

"I can do that," Bull said. "Just wanted to have me some fun, sort of get even."

"And get outsmarted, you mean." Arms folded across his chest, Amos Gordon studied the big redhead for a long minute. Then, "All right, Bull. I'll leave it up to you, long as you do it like I've told you. Billy Jay'll go along just for luck."

"I won't be needing no help."

"Maybe not, but I ain't taking no chances on letting something mess up a good thing. . . . Now, a couple of you truss him up."

"Could take him up there now," Turnbull

said, glancing through the doorway. "Still light."

"Nope, be dark time you got there, and trying to do something like that when you can't see so good leads to trouble. He'll keep."

Billy Jay and Roder pulled themselves upright. The gunman turned to his saddlebags, dug out several strips of rawhide, and then together the pair crossed to where Shawn hunched.

"Put your hands behind you," the younger man directed.

Starbuck complied, said, "Like to ask one question, satisfy my curiosity."

Gordon bobbed his head. "Guess you're entitled to that. What's the question?"

"You kill Damon Friend and throw him down that mine shaft, too?"

The outlaw spat, brushed at his lips. "Nope, we ain't had nothing to do with him. Fact is, we didn't start working our deal until after he'd took off. Guess you could say he sort of give us the idea. Why, he something to you?"

"I'm starting to think he is," Linden said, coming into the conversation. "Been asking all kinds of questions about him ever since he showed up."

Gordon squinted at Shawn. "Could be

he's some sort of a lawman?"

"Claims he ain't."

"What he claims and what is could be something different. See what you can find on him, Cliff."

Roder, jerking Shawn roughly about, went through his pockets. After it was over, he returned to the others.

"Ain't nothing much. Few dollars. No badge or papers saying he's a lawman."

"Well, no matter," the drummer said, losing interest. "Won't change anything one way or another. Get him tied up so's we can set down and divvy up this gold. . . . You still set on pulling out, Dan?"

Roder, assisted by Billy Jay, applied the lengths of rawhide to Shawn's wrists and ankles, pushed him back into the corner, and then hurriedly rejoined their friends at the blanket.

Starbuck watched them settle down on the floor, take their places in the circle. One thing he had learned for sure, Ben hadn't fallen victim to them. He had already taken the twenty thousand and gone when they began their operation, according to Gordon. It was good to know that much — even if it wasn't likely to do him any good.

"Sure ain't much when you split it up five ways," Turnbull grumbled, stacking his share of the ingots before him.

"Why we ain't taking no chance on fouling things up," Gordon said, turning one of the small, shining blocks over and over in his stubby hands. "Going to take a bit of time to get a stake built up — leastwise, one the size I'm aiming to get before I move on."

"Well, I've got all I need," Dan Linden said. "Enough here for me to do all I've got in mind." His voice was flat, listless. Turnbull looked at him closely.

"You still mooning about having to stick a knife into that driver?"

Linden scraped idly at one of the ingots with a fingernail. "Otey was all right. Sure hated doing it."

"Man always has to pay a price of some kind to get what he wants," Gordon said. "You sure you want to go? Could probably double what you got there if you'd hang around for another month or so."

"This is all I'll need," Linden replied. "Ought to bring somewhere close to twenty-five hundred dollars."

"Maybe even three thousand," Billy Jay said.

"Most likely," Gordon agreed, leaning back. "Only thing, be damned sure you scratch that Skull mold mark off the bottom. You don't want some banker —"

"Figuring on melting it down again, pouring my own bars. Friend I know's got a furnace."

"He keep his mouth shut?" Gordon asked, frowning.

"Sure will — long as he gets paid."

"Good. Just might be interested in doing business with him myself —"

"Not me," Turnbull interrupted, stroking one of the ingots gently, almost lovingly. "Ain't giving away none of what I've got. Way I see it, it won't be such easy pickings from here on. What with Skull losing two big hauls, and the other mines getting took too, and then the Army moving in — it's going to get mighty touchy."

"Ain't no doubt," Gordon said. "And to do any good, we're going to have to find us another inside like Dan. Sure does help when we know one of the outfits is making a big shipment."

Turnbull laughed, jerked his head at Shawn. "Just come to me. The Skull bunch is going to think this here new outrider of theirs hightailed it with this shipment just like that other jasper, Friend, did!"

Billy Jay joined in the laughter. "Bet they will at that! With the driver dead, and them thinking Dan . . ."

Starbuck, working steadily if futilely at loosening the cord binding his wrists together, only half-heard what was being said. He could learn nothing from them, he realized; they, like everyone else, believed that Ben had stolen the gold and fled the country.

Roder yawned, began to pick up his share of the ingots, stuff them into a pair of saddlebags. The others followed suit. It was almost dark inside the cabin, but no one made a move to light the lantern; either there was no plan to do so or it was out of oil.

"We going to have to keep a watch on him?" Billy Jay asked, rising and pointing at Starbuck.

The onetime whiskey drummer slung his saddlebags over his shoulder, crossed to where Shawn lay, and carefully examined the buckskin bindings. He shook his head.

"Naw, he ain't going nowhere. But just to be sure, I'll do my sleeping in the doorway. He ain't going to get by me."

18

It was a long, uncomfortable night for Starbuck, one in which he continued to twist and pull at the rawhide locking his wrists together in the hopes of slipping the bonds. Near dawn he gave it up. If he was to escape the death the outlaws planned for him, he would have to accomplish it at some time during the trip to the mine shaft Gordon had spoken of, or else after they had reached there.

He slept briefly, awoke to the sound of the men stirring about. Stiff, he watched them go out into the yard, heard their sour mutterings and complaints. Shortly the smell of brewing coffee came to him, mingled with the odor of burning greasewood. Later he could hear them in low conversation as they satisfied their hunger.

He had given up on being accorded a ration of food and coffee when Dan Linden appeared in the doorway carrying a tin cup of the steaming liquid. He set it down on the dusty floor near Shawn, drew his pistol.

"Rest of the boys don't see no sense in wasting grub on you, but I figured you oughta at least have a cup of coffee."

"Obliged," Starbuck said, glancing through the doorway at the other men. . . . Even if he got the chance to make a break, he'd never get by them.

"I'm untying your hands so's you can drink it. Warning you now, don't try nothing cute."

Starbuck shrugged. "With the whole bunch just outside — what could I do?"

He leaned forward, allowed Linden to get at the rawhide strip. When it came loose, he immediately began to chafe his wrists, restore circulation. Linden waited a few moments, nodded.

"Now, hold them out in front so's I can tie them together again."

Shawn frowned. "Thought you said you'd —"

"You can hold the cup with them tied," the outlaw said, and linked Starbuck's wrists once more. Finished, he picked up the cup, placed it in Shawn's cupped hands.

"I'll be watching," he said, moving toward the door. "Don't try nothing."

Starbuck took a swallow of the brew. It

was strong, black, and exactly what he needed. Eyes on the men moving about in the yard, he continued to sip at the cup. A ray of hope had lifted within him. With hands tied in front of him, chances for escape were enhanced many times over, but any effort must wait until he was on the trail with Bull and Billy Jay; he'd have no chance now against so many. All he could do now was wait — and pray they did not again pin his arms behind him.

Finished with the coffee, he let the cup fall to the floor. Immediately Turnbull stepped up to the doorway, glanced in. He studied Starbuck briefly, turned away.

"Reckon we'd better take care of him," he said.

Someone made an answering comment, but the words were lost to Shawn. Shortly Billy Jay asked, "What'll we do with his horse? He ain't no scrub like them others, and if we turn him loose, somebody's bound to recognize him."

"Sure is a mighty fine-looking animal," Cliff Roder remarked. "Wouldn't mind keeping him for myself."

"And right quick get yourself hung for horse stealing!" Gordon said in a disgusted voice.

"How, with him dead?"

"Be a few folks around here who'll remember that sorrel and that he belonged to Starbuck, or whatever his name is. When he shows up missing and you turn up on his horse, what's people going to think?

"That you had something to do with him disappearing, that's what, and then they'll start talking murder, and the Army'll step in. Damnit, Cliff, I ain't sure you got —"

"You mean you want us to throw him down that shaft, too?" Billy Jay cut in. "Hell, big as he is, it'll be a mighty hard job."

Gordon spat. "No, don't mean for you to do that," he said wearily. "Drive him off into one of them back canyons and shoot him. Coyotes and buzzards'll do the rest. And you'd best get started, all right. Somebody might come along, and we don't want them seeing him."

A short time later Billy Jay entered the shack, crossed to Shawn's side. Hooking a hand under an armpit, he said, "Come on, mister, we're going," and helped Starbuck to rise.

The outlaw frowned, looked down at Shawn's bound ankles. "He can't do no walking or setting a saddle with his feet tied up," he called through the doorway.

"Then cut them loose," Gordon shouted back. "You're going to be standing right beside him with your gun in your hand, ain't you?"

Billy Jay drew his pistol, said, "Just what I'm doing."

Moving around behind Starbuck, he dug into his pocket for a jackknife, opened a blade with his teeth, and bending down, severed the rawhide cords.

"Now, walk out that there door," the young outlaw ordered, "and climb on your horse. Don't try nothing."

"Be a fool to," Shawn answered. So far there had been nothing said about changing the position of his hands.

Blinking in the strong sunlight, holding tight to his one bit of hope, Starbuck stepped out into the yard. The sorrel had been found by the outlaws, now waited for him. He crossed to the big gelding slowly, and hooking his hands about the saddle-horn, thrust a foot into a stirrup and swung aboard.

At once Turnbull moved up, coiled rope in his hands. Shaking out a loop, he dropped it around Shawn, yanked it tight. Allowing no slack, he crossed to his horse. Billy Jay was already astride his mount, pistol yet in hand.

"Won't be needing that for a spell," the redhead said, going onto the saddle. "This here lariat'll keep him behaving."

"Best you play it safe," the drummer cautioned. "One of you ride in front, other'n stay in behind. I don't trust him much."

"What can he do?" Turnbull demanded impatiently. "Hands are tied, and if he jumps off the saddle, this rope'll catch him up fast. Wouldn't mind dragging him over the rocks for a ways."

Gordon stirred resignedly. "Suit yourself — just don't screw it up."

"Don't worry none," Billy Jay said as they cut about and moved off toward the trail. "This here jasper's taking his last ride."

Turnbull, a dozen strides ahead as they started up the slope, kept the rope taut. Shawn, arms pinned to his sides, sat rigidly on the sorrel. He needed to create enough slack in the lariat to permit movement if he was to get at the knife in his boot, and with Billy Jay following Gordon's suggestion and riding behind him, he was finding it difficult to do anything without drawing the outlaw's attention. But he worked at it, nevertheless, doing it stealthily and moving his shoulders as little as possible.

Luck abruptly favored him. Bull Turnbull reached back, dug into his saddlebags, came up with a half-full bottle of whiskey. Twisting about, he held it aloft for Billy Jay to see.

"Come on up here," he called. "Got something a mite stronger'n that coffee Cliff made."

The young outlaw spurred past Starbuck at once, swung in beside the redhead without looking back. Instantly Shawn flexed his arms, loosened the rope, leaning forward as he did so that no pull would be noticed by Turnbull.

With the loop slack, he bent lower, and with linked hands working together, reached into his left boot. Locking stiff fingers about the handle of the blade, he drew himself upright, brought the knife into the clear.

Hastily placing his hands in his lap, and shielded somewhat by the saddlehorn, he carefully reversed the razor-sharp weapon, and wedging the handle under his leg, began to saw at the rawhide. Within moments the cord parted.

Heaving a sigh of relief, he glanced ahead. The two outlaws were passing the bottle back and forth, laughing and talking as they moved steadily up the trail. Shawn snugged the rope tight about his body once more, leaving the knife hidden under his leg. He had no exact plan of action, had thought only to the point of getting the blade and freeing his hands, but whatever, it must wait until they had traveled a longer distance from the shack. A gunshot would attract the remaining outlaws instantly.

They rode on, climbing out onto another ridge, dropping into a second valley, this one narrow and deep and more of a canyon. The bottle became empty, was tossed away, to shatter noisily on the rocks below. When they reached the floor of the gash, Turnbull looked over his shoulder. His face was flushed, and his mouth split into a wide grin.

"Ain't far now, dude!" he called.

Soon they broke out into a small clearing just above the level of the canyon's floor. In the side of the hill, near its center, Starbuck could see an opening, one not much larger than a man's body. Rotting framework close by, jutting out at odd angles, indicated the collapse of the shaft's entrance.

"That there's your grave!" Billy Jay said, pointing at the small gap.

"Yeh, about a hundred feet down," the redhead added, and laughed.

It was now or not at all, Shawn decided. If he waited until the pair had halted, his chances would be greatly reduced. Raising his arms, he caught the rope in one hand, and clutching the knife in the other, drove his spurs into the sorrel's flanks. Startled, the big gelding lunged forward, swerved to avoid a collision with the two animals in front of him.

Turnbull yelled, tried to wheel. The rope, going taut as the sorrel whipped by Billy Jay, jerked him partly off the saddle. Starbuck, launching himself at the younger outlaw, drove his knife into the man's chest and dragged him to the ground.

They struck with a solid thud, a groan breaking from the outlaw's flared mouth. He was dead or dying, and Starbuck, clawing the weapon from the man's holster, rocked back, fired hurriedly at Bull Turnbull, balance recovered and bringing up his own weapon.

The reports blended as one. Shawn saw Billy Jay's lifeless body jolt as the bullet meant for him missed, hit the dead outlaw. He triggered a second shot at Turnbull, looming over him. It was unnecessary. The redhead, mouth gaping, face drawn into contorted lines, was buckling slowly. The follow-up bullet only hastened his fall to the ground.

19

Sucking for breath, Starbuck pulled himself upright. He stood for a time staring at Turnbull and Billy Jay, stilled as always by the utter finality of such unbridled moments; and then, sliding the pistol he had taken from the outlaw into his holster, he crossed to where the redhead lay, knelt, and made a quick examination. Turnbull was dead; he knew that, but had to make sure. At such times it was only prudent to take nothing for granted.

Pivoting, he moved to Billy Jay. He also was dead. Reaching down, Starbuck picked up the knife where he had dropped it, whetted the dark stain from the blade by thrusting it into the sandy soil several times, and returned it to its scabbard in his boot.

That done, he brought up the outlaws' horses, loaded the bodies across the saddles, and secured them. Then, using the lariat Bull Turnbull had employed to lead him into the canyon, Shawn linked the two horses together, and mounting his sorrel, headed back for the cabin and the remaining outlaws.

Restraint continued its grip upon him for some time, and that lonely emptiness that filled him after such occasions was as a heavy cloak. Outlaws or not, to be a party to death never set well with him, even though it came about in the process of protecting his own life. And it wasn't over yet. He still had three more desperate men, all willing killers, to deal with. He could only hope they would not resist but surrender.

By the time he reached the ridge overlooking the shack, the feeling within him had dissipated somewhat, and moving down the trail slowly, he made a quiet approach to the clearing. That the gunshots might have been heard by Gordon and the others did not matter, since they would have come from the distance and would have been considered to be only an indication that Turnbull and Billy Jay had completed the task they had been assigned to do.

Taking no chance, Starbuck pulled to a halt in the deep brush well above the cabin, and tethering the horses, moved in silently on foot. He was carrying the guns he had taken from the outlaws, both old, worn weapons that had a heavy, uncomfortable feel; he would have traded the pair instantly for his own weapon, still in Gordon's possession. But they were just as deadly as his forty-five, and since he would be going up against three men, it would be an advantage to have a pistol in each hand.

He heard their voices moments before he reached the edge of the yard. Hunched low, he worked in close, paused. They were squatting around a saddle blanket, near the dead fire, playing three-handed poker. None seemed particularly interested in the game, and it was evident they were simply passing time until their two friends returned. Close by, the horses, saddled and ready for departure, waited.

Starbuck moved to his left until he was at a more advantageous point. He watched the outlaws for another brief time; and then, pistols leveled, he stepped into the open. Linden was the only one in the party facing into Shawn's direction. His head came up in surprise; his mouth sagged.

"Raise your hands — high!"

At Starbuck's sharp command, Roder and Gordon stiffened. Linden, finding his voice, stammered, "It's . . . it's him!"

"On your feet! Do it slow."

The outlaws obeyed silently. Shawn moved in close, plucked the revolvers from their holsters, not overlooking the one Cliff Roder carried under his waistband. Reclaiming his own, he tossed the others far out into the brush. It had gone easier than he'd anticipated, he thought as he circled around to where he could face all three. Amos Gordon met his glance with glittering eyes.

"Bull and Billy Jay —"

"Hanging across their saddles."

The outlaw chief cursed vividly. "Might've known that bastard would mess it up! Can't depend no —"

"I'm taking you in to Wickenburg," Starbuck cut in coldly. "You can go sitting up on your horse or tied over the saddle, like them. Leaving it up to you."

Dan Linden sighed hopelessly. "Never no luck," he murmured in a lost voice. "Just never could have no luck."

"Luck's something a man makes for himself," Gordon snapped, "so don't go bawling to somebody else about it. And I expect yours has flat run out for sure — it being you that knifed that teamster. . . . Want you remembering that, Starbuck; was Linden here that killed Cooper."

Shawn, ignoring the outlaw, motioned to

179

Cliff Roder. "It was you that had some rawhide thongs in your saddle-bags last night. Let's see if you can find some more — without getting yourself shot."

The gunman's jaw tightened, but he moved to one of the horses, unbuckled a saddlebag, and produced several strips of the leather. Sullen, he returned to Starbuck, passed them over.

Shawn nodded crisply to Linden and Gordon. "Put your hands behind you."

The men complied, and Roder, under Starbuck's direction and close surveillance, bound their wrists and then stood quietly while his own were lashed together by the tall rider.

"Like to ask a favor," he said in a low voice as the knot was being drawn tight. "I ain't exactly what folks believe I am. A gunman, I mean. This here's the first big trouble I ever got in, and if you'll —"

"Save it for the judge," Shawn advised, and appropriating one of the lariats, formed three loops at proper intervals, dropped them over the outlaws' heads, and settled them snugly about their necks. One by one he assisted them to mount, and stepped back.

"Aim to tie this end to my saddle," he said, holding up the rope. "No need telling you that if you try to run for it you'll save the territory the expense of a trial and hanging."

The outlaws made no reply, and backtracking to where the sorrel and the other horses with their grisly loads waited, Shawn climbed aboard the gelding and struck for Wickenburg.

His entrance drew instant attention. With three captive riders strung out ahead of him, each linked to the other with a rope that encircled his neck, and trailing two more hung across their saddles, almost the entire population had gathered about him by the time he had pulled up to the jail tree in the square — all shouting questions at the same time, it seemed.

Constable Leyman shouldered his way through the crowd as Starbuck dismounted. He glanced at the prisoners, looked close at the dead men, and faced Shawn.

"What's this all about?"

"They're the ones that held up Skull's wagon yesterday and killed Otey Cooper," Starbuck replied, and gave the details of the incident and capture. When he had finished, the lawman nodded.

"Had a posse out hunting them — and you," he said. "Just about made up our minds that them Skull people had lost another shipment."

"Gold's all here," Shawn said. "I'll take it to Wells Fargo, get a receipt. Will you take charge of these men?"

"Can bet I will!" Leyman said. "Judge'll be here in a couple of days, and they'll be waiting under the tree for him. Them dead ones — there's room in the boneyard for them."

Starbuck turned, moved along the horses, and collected the saddlebags, each containing a portion of the gold ingots. Draping them over his shoulders, he pushed through the still-gathered crowd, crossed the street to the stage company's quarters, and turned the pouches over to the agent, watching the proceedings from the doorway.

"Heard you talking," the man said, laying the bags out on the counter and tugging at the straps and buckles. "Won't take me but a couple of minutes to fix you up — then you can get back out there. . . . Bet there's a lot of folks wanting to buy you a drink."

"They can save their money," Shawn replied, and crossed to the barred window. The gathering around the jail had not decreased, now was avidly watching as Leyman affixed the cuffs with their lengths of heavy chains to the three outlaws. The horses with Turnbull and Billy Jay slung across the saddles still waited in the hot sunlight.

"The Skull people ought to be mighty grateful to you," the agent said, filling out the receipt. "Was lucky you were around to save their gold."

Starbuck shrugged. "What I was hired to do. Part I hate about it is it cost Otey Cooper his life."

"Yeh, too bad. Which one of that bunch done it?"

"Linden," Shawn answered. "But they were all in on it. Had it planned out."

"Five of them — mighty lucky for you, too, that you didn't get a bullet."

"Wasn't because they didn't try," Starbuck said grimly, taking the slip of paper.

The Wells Fargo man slapped his hands together. "Well, like I said, it's working out good for Skull. You saved this shipment for them, and that fellow Friend, the man that got away with the other big shipment, has been spotted in Tucson."

20

Shawn drew up slowly. "You dead sure of that?"

The agent's brows lifted. "Reckon I am. Drummer rode in this morning. Hadn't heard about the robbery. When he did, he come straight to me, told me Friend was in Tucson. Said he'd seen him there not more'n four or five days ago."

"There any chance he could be wrong?"

"None. He's been doing business with Skull for years. Seen Friend plenty of times. . . . That's where he is now, at the mine, talking to Truxton and Nix. Sent him right on out there soon's I heard what he had to say."

Starbuck mulled over the information in silence. It was a relief to hear that Ben was alive — but being alive and seen meant that Skull would notify the law to move in, arrest him for the theft of the gold that had been in his charge, as well as the murder of the man they called Jamie.

It seemed a bit strange that Ben would take the risk of hanging around Tucson and not hurry on across the border to safety in Mexico, since the old mission town was only a three- or four-day ride distant.

Again doubt as to his brother's guilt rose in Shawn's mind, and despite all of the so-called proof that had to be considered, the reluctance to believe Ben had committed the crimes was now stronger than ever.

Abruptly he wheeled, stepped through the doorway into the hot sunlight, and crossed to the sorrel. The crowd yet hovered around the jail tree talking with the prisoners, asking questions, hoorawing them, voicing threats. Someone had finally led off the horses carrying the bodies of Bull Turnbull and Billy Jay.

Mounting, Shawn rode hurriedly out of town and made the return ride to the crusher camp at a steady gallop. If Truxton hadn't sent a message to the Tucson law authorities, he would volunteer to carry it; getting to Ben first, affording him the opportunity to deny the charges lodged against him — or to admit them if they were true — before involving any lawman would be important.

He swung directly to the foreman's office

upon reaching the grounds, dropped from the saddle, and entered. The room was empty. Swearing, he turned to the door, looked out into the yard for some sign of the man. He was not to be seen, but the blacksmith and two other employees were trotting toward him, features showing surprise.

"We all figured you'd took off," the smithy said as they halted. "Like that —"

Shawn held up the Wells Fargo receipt. "Gold's been turned in to the stage company," he said, reaching back and pinning the slip of paper on a spindle. "Where's Truxton?"

"Drummer come here saying that fellow Friend was in Tucson. He and John went up to the mine to tell Aaron. You see anything of Dan Linden?"

"Constable's got him chained up, along with the rest of the gang that killed Otey Cooper and held up the wagon," Shawn said. "You know if Truxton sent a man to Tucson to talk to the law about Friend?"

"Don't think so — not from here, anyway. Expect it'll be Aaron doing that."

Such was probably true. The foreman was not likely to act without first reporting to and consulting with Aaron Nix, the superintendent. In the process, two or three hours would be consumed. That was a break; if he moved fast, he might still be able to get to Ben ahead of the law.

"Was sure a shame about Otey. . . ."

Starbuck nodded to the blacksmith. "Was a fine fellow," he said, turning to the sorrel. "But the man who did it will pay for it."

"That's good."

"If I don't see Truxton, tell him about the receipt I put on his table."

"Why — you quitting?"

"Making a little trip. Ought to be back in a few days," Shawn answered, and moved on across the yard to his quarters.

Leaving the sorrel ground-reined, he entered, hurriedly began to collect his belongings. Rushing to warn Ben of his impending danger from the law wasn't exactly the reunion with his brother he'd envisioned. Before, it had been a matter of finding him, enjoying the meeting, and then explaining that it was necessary they both return to Ohio so that the will of old Hiram could be satisfied.

Their father had forgiven his elder son for running away and wanted him to share in his estate; but locating him and bringing this about was a chore he had left up to Shawn, making it clear that the small fortune safely stashed away in a bank was not to be touched until both sons were there to share equally. In the fulfillment of this, Starbuck had covered many miles, had often been close but had never quite caught up to Ben. Now it seemed he was about to complete the quest — only it would be under far different circumstances than expected.

"I'm glad you're back."

Shawn paused, swore under his breath. Cassie Truxton. At the moment, she was about the last person he cared to see. He turned to her. She was dressed in boots, corduroy riding skirt, heavy blouse, and wide-brimmed hat. Nodding, he resumed the rolling of his blanket and extra clothing into a tight cylinder.

"John and some of the others thought you had thrown in with outlaws — stolen the shipment of gold. I wouldn't believe it. I was sure you'd return."

"Thanks," he said dryly.

"What happened?"

He gave her a brief accounting of the robbery and the capture of the outlaws. She was quiet for a time, and then: "Now you're leaving. . . . Tucson?"

"Maybe."

Cassie came farther into the room. "I know that's where you're going. I heard what that drummer had to say about Damon."

"So . . . ?"

"You're going there to see him." Again she was silent. Finally, "He's your brother, isn't he?"

Starbuck shrugged. "Could be."

"You're going there to warn him before the law can find him."

"Aim to see him, but not just about that. Not sure he's guilty of stealing that gold. If he is, I'll try to talk him into giving it back."

Cassie nodded. "I knew there was something — all those questions you asked, your taking his old job, and looking alike. . . . I'm going with you."

He spun to her angrily. "The hell you are! I've got problems enough without taking on yours."

"My problems are over, and I could help you hunt for him."

"That'll be no chore. Tucson's not all that big."

She smiled. "Suit yourself. Fact is, I'm going anyway. Started getting things ready as soon as John rode out to see Aaron Nix. I just thought it would be nice if we rode together."

"What about Truxton?"

"I'm leaving him — for good. Made up

my mind to that the other day, and now that I know where Damon is, it's settled."

"You've tried going before, and he always brought you back."

"It's different this time. He'll never bring me back. . . . Never!"

Shawn finished assembling his gear, and moving out to the waiting sorrel, secured it to the saddle. There wasn't time to spare for laying in a supply of trail grub. He would have to depend on what little he had on hand and what could be obtained along the way.

Ready, he turned to the girl. She was standing in the doorway, leaning against the frame. There was a quiet set to her features.

"Like to help you," he said, gentling his words, "but it's important I get there before Nix notifies the law. Means I'll be traveling hard."

Her shoulders stirred slightly. "I wouldn't hold you back."

"Maybe not," Starbuck said, stepping into the saddle and pulling away. "Just can't chance it. . . . *Adios.*"

21

Starbuck cut due south from the crusher camp, bypassing Wickenburg and taking a trail that roughly paralleled the Hassayampa River. Tucson lay more to the east, but there were advantages to following the better route along the water, and later he could correct his course without any undue loss of time. As long as he stayed on the near side of the Maricopa Mountains, he knew he would be all right.

He was feeling a bit sorry now that he had been so short with Cassie Truxton. He could have let her down a bit easier by making a fuller explanation of his reasons, he realized, but the need to be on his way, with nothing occupying his thoughts other than Ben, was uppermost in his mind. Had he agreed to let her accompany him, he would only be inviting trouble and delay, for there was little doubt that John Truxton, returning from the mine and finding her gone, would immediately set out in pursuit.

Cassie would be all right. Chances were she had given up the idea of making the long trip to Tucson when she learned she would have to go it alone.

A time later, as the sorrel moved tirelessly along, it occurred to Shawn that he had missed several meals. He had fully intended to get himself breakfast that morning after delivering his prisoners to Wickenburg's Constable Leyman, but the news passed to him by the Wells Fargo agent concerning Ben drove the need from his mind.

Turning, he glanced at the sun. Several hours yet until dark. He'd keep moving for a while yet before making camp. He could then boil up a can of coffee and make a meal on it and the few hard biscuits and strips of jerky that were in his saddlebags. Tomorrow he'd keep his eyes peeled for a ranch or homestead, or perhaps a mining camp, where he could buy some food. In the meantime he'd be on the alert for a cottontail or a squirrel to fill in with.

Near dark, with the sorrel showing signs of wear, Starbuck pulled up in a brushy cove not far from the river but a reasonable distance off the trail. Stripping the gear from the gelding and seeing to the horse's needs first, he then set about satisfying his own wants.

It was Apache country, and it was only wise to make himself as inconspicuous as possible. The screened location he had chosen, removed as it was from the path, would permit him to go unnoticed by passing riders unless their attention was drawn to him for some cause. For that reason he debated the advisability of building a fire to make coffee, ruled against it. Better to settle for water, and safety; he could make coffee in the morning, and then if the smell of smoke drew any curious braves, he would be gone by the time they located the source of the odor.

Seated on his blanket, gear nearby, he ate the two rock-solid biscuits and chewed on the salty, dry beef his flour-sack larder had provided, and gradually dulled his hunger. Tomorrow he'd do better; he'd had no luck along the trail insofar as small animals were concerned, which was just as well, he guessed — a gunshot certainly would have notified all the Apaches in the area of his presence, and he was doing his best to avoid that. But it wasn't the first time he'd gone hungry — and likely it wasn't the last.

Returning what was left of the jerky to the sack, he stowed it away, and rising, went for a final look at the sorrel. He was feeling the weight of weariness himself now, something that was not unexpected, as he had gotten very little sleep during that previous night, when the outlaws had held him prisoner in the shack, and he had been on the move every minute since daylight.

The sorrel was munching contentedly on the bunch grass and other ground growth; taking up the picket rope, Shawn led the big horse to the stream for a final drink. That done, he returned the gelding to his pasturing and once again settled down on the blanket.

The dry swish of a disturbed branch somewhere on the trail brought Starbuck to quick attention. Drawing his pistol, he moved to the edge of the brush. Crouched low, he waited, eyes riveted to the opposite side of the clearing. A moment later a horse appeared, a small bay or black carrying a slightly built rider. It was not an Apache, he saw, easing back, and then he swore quietly as the pilgrim came farther into the open. It was Cassie Truxton.

She had done as she had said she would do — head for Tucson with or without him; his refusal to permit her accompanying him had brought about no reconsideration of her intentions. Evidently she meant to break with Truxton this time.

He watched her move by in silence, still reluctant to saddle himself with her and her problems, yet knowing that he could not allow her to make the dangerous journey alone regardless of who she was or what the circumstances involved.

Rising, he called out softly, "Cassie."

The girl halted instantly, a faint cry bursting from her lips. Starbuck stepped into the open.

"Over here," he said. He had tried not to startle her, had failed.

She brought the black around, came toward him, fear draining from her features. "I . . . I thought I'd missed you, somehow," she murmured, relief filling her voice.

He stared at her. "You trailing me?"

"Yes . . . or, I mean, I was," she answered, coming off the mare. "I lost your tracks when it got dark — I thought I'd catch up with you before then." She glanced around. "Where are you camped?"

He pointed to the far side of the brush. "In there," he said, and taking the black's reins, led the horse to where the sorrel was picketed.

"Don't you have a fire? I'm cold. . . ."

"No," he said as he began to strip the mare. "Be the same as asking every Apache in the country to drop by."

Cassie looked off into the moonlight-flooded night. "I never saw any. . . ."

"Neither did I, but they're around. Didn't that little fracas with those three the other day teach you anything?"

She stepped back as he entered the coulee with her gear. "Just an accident."

"Not exactly," he said, handing her the blanket he'd removed from the cantle of her saddle. "Been told the Apaches have a habit of hanging around in the hills here waiting for the chance to jump pilgrims — especially the ones traveling alone."

"I haven't got anything they'd want — no money, no gold."

"Not what they're after. It's your horse and gun, if you've got one."

She nodded, patted the pocket of her jacket. "My derringer. John gave it to me when we were first married. I've learned to shoot it."

"Wrong kind of gun for out here," Shawn said. "You hungry?"

Cassie shook her head. "No, I ate a little along the way. . . . Coffee would taste good, though."

"Have to wait till morning," he said gruffly.

Cassie's shoulders stirred faintly, and moving to where he had dropped her saddle, she spread her blanket on the ground. Sitting down, she looked at him, her face a pale oval in the night.

"I won't be any trouble. I promise."

Shawn felt the angry resentment within him cool. He guessed he shouldn't be so hard on her — nor should he be one to judge her actions. If Ben meant so much to her that she would give up all she had, however small, and undertake a long and danger-filled journey to be with him, it was not his right to censure her or say she was wrong. But there was no denying there could be complications, and he'd best be prepared.

"Your husband," he said, dropping onto his own blanket, "does he know you've left him again?"

"By now. He hadn't come back from the mine when I rode out."

"Anybody see you leave?"

"I suppose. There's damned little I've ever been able to do around there that someone hasn't seen and reported to him."

"He'll be coming after you. Expect you know that."

The girl sighed, brushed at the wrinkles in her jacket front. "Maybe this time he won't. I think he's finally realized it's hopeless."

Yawning, Shawn lay back on his blanket.

He'd like to believe what she had said was the way it would be, but recalling Truxton's actions and words, he had doubts. He yawned again, the need for sleep growing stronger.

"Are you really Damon's brother?"

He shifted. "Yeh. His real name's Ben — and Starbuck, same as mine. I've been trying to find him for a long time."

"Why? What has he done?"

"Nothing — just a family matter. Can clear it up quick, once we get together."

"Something he did?"

"Not the way you mean, I expect. He ran off from home when he was a boy. Been a little over ten years ago. Needs to go back with me to settle our pa's estate."

"I see," she murmured. "Ben Starbuck. . . . It's a nice name. I don't think I ever heard yours — the first part."

"Shawn."

She repeated the word, said, "It's sort of strange, but nice, too."

Starbuck fell silent again, his mind now considering a question that had occurred to him before; if Ben thought so much of Cassie, why had he not sent for her? That he had not taken her with him at the start was understandable, since the decision to steal Skull's gold, if indeed he had done so, neither called for outside distractions nor afforded opportunity for them.

But later, after the lapse of time, it seemed logical he would have managed somehow to get word to her. That he felt secure was proven by the fact that he apparently moved freely about in Tucson.

"You sure Ben will be looking for you?" It was a delicate question, and he put it as best he could.

Her reply was prompt. "Of course! Why wouldn't he?"

"Seems like he would have gotten in touch with you."

"Probably would have in a few more days. My coming on will save all that."

Shawn hoped she was right — for her sake. After a bit he said, "Think you ought to know I aim to talk Ben into returning that gold when I see him — if he stole it. That make any difference to you?"

Cassie was silent for a long minute. Then, "It would be nice to have a lot of money. Always wanted that kind of life — being able to do all the things I've dreamed of, buy what I wanted, live like a real lady. But it doesn't matter now. It's Damon — Ben — that I want to be with. Nothing else counts."

Starbuck pulled the blanket about himself,

adjusted his head on the saddle-blanket pillow. "Glad to hear you say that. Thought maybe it was mostly the money."

Her reply was faintly angry. "You don't think much of me, do you?"

"Don't know you, and what little I've seen hasn't scored too high in my book," he said bluntly.

Strangely, that did not heighten her anger. "I guess I gave you plenty of reason to feel that way. But John — something about him makes me act that way. I've reached the point, I suppose, where I will do about anything to aggravate him, make him mad."

"Well, let's hope that's done with now," Shawn said wearily. "Best we get some sleep. Tomorrow'll be a long, hard day."

"Good night. . . ."

He heard her voice faintly, muttered a response, and rolled onto his side. In only moments, it seemed, he became aware of daylight.

22

Starbuck sat up. Cassie, carrying an armload of dry branches, was just entering the coulee. She saw him, smiled.

"Thought I'd get things started."

He nodded, came to his feet. Taking the wood from her, he began to lay a small fire. He had hoped to get back on the trail much earlier, but reckoned there was no great harm done.

Cassie moved by him to his saddle, apparently assuming he had come well provisioned, and opening his saddlebags, obtained the flour sack of supplies. Taking out the lard tin used to make coffee and pouring in a quantity of crushed beans, she added water from the canteen and placed the container on the rocks he had grouped about the flames.

Again she took up the sack, looked into it, frowned. "What do we eat?"

"Jerky and coffee," he said. "All I've got

until we find a place where I can do a little buying."

The girl turned to her own gear, procured a sack of her own. "There's plenty here," she said, setting it beside him. "Brought bacon, some soda crackers, bread, a few potatoes."

Starbuck looked up at her, grinned. "Going to be a big help. It'll save us time," he said, and digging a frying pan out of his saddlebags, sliced a quantity of the bacon and a couple of the potatoes into it. Enlarging the circle of rocks enclosing the fire, he put the food to cooking.

"Soon as that's done, we can fry up a little of the bread in the grease. You handle it?"

Cassie took the knife he offered her. "Of course," she replied, puzzled.

"While you're doing that, I'll get the horses ready to go. Have to pull out soon as we've eaten."

"Apaches?"

"Mostly," he replied, and picking up their gear, carried it to where the horses were picketed.

By the time he had their mounts saddled and bridled, Cassie was calling him to breakfast. He hunkered beside her, quickly ate his portions and drank his share of the strong coffee. Finished, he at once began to collect the remaining gear and store it in its proper place.

Cassie watched him, sipping slowly at her tin of steaming liquid. He glanced impatiently at her.

"Best we get out of here."

She rose, tossed the last few drops of liquid into the dead fire. "I don't think it's just the Apaches you're in such a hurry over. . . ."

"You're right," he snapped. "I'm thinking about your husband, too. Looked for him to show up during the night. Probably means he got started late and's not far behind us now."

"There's nothing he can do."

"He can slow us down — and that's what I don't want. If I don't get to Tucson ahead of the man Aaron Nix is sending to swear out a warrant for Ben, I'll be too late to help him."

Cassie's attitude changed perceptibly. "I . . . I never thought of that," she said, and hurried to the black. "Is there anything I can do?"

"All done," he answered, buckling his saddlebags. "Can fill the canteens when we water the horses, later on."

She swung onto the mare, settled herself. Shawn took a final look around, satisfied himself that they were leaving nothing behind, and also went to the saddle. Cutting the sorrel about, he crossed the clearing and rejoined the trail.

They rode southward for an hour or so at a good pace, and then, as the brush thickened and the going became slower, Starbuck slowed the gelding. Their night camp was now well in the distance, and if any Apaches had been drawn to it, they would pose no danger.

The trail pushed on, weaving in and out of dense growth, cutting across open meadows, rising and falling with the short hills and shallow valleys. Near noon they broke out onto a broad flat with a ridge of low-lying mountains to their right. Heat was by now becoming a factor, and Shawn accordingly veered toward the hills, which, while mostly barren rock, did exhibit an occasional patch of brush and resulting shade.

Gaining the ragged formations, they continued for a time and then drew to a halt. There was no stream apparent, and they satisfied their thirst from the supply they carried. Their horses were not in need and could wait until later, when, hopefully, they would reach another stream or spring.

"In all the time you've been looking for your brother, haven't you ever seen him?"

Cassie asked as they rested in the filigreed shadow of a paloverde tree.

Shawn brushed at the sweat on his face. "Never have. Always just a jump behind him — a day late. Not even sure I'll know him when I see him. . . . Been told we look alike, but that's not much help. Person never actually knows what he looks like."

Cassie smiled. "I guess that's true where a man's concerned. Different with a woman. . . . There is a resemblance, all right. You're taller. Damon has darker eyes — more blue than yours — but the face is pretty much the same."

She had called Ben by the name he had assumed, had done so several times earlier. Likely she always would. Again he wondered if his brother thought as much of the girl as she did of him. It was very probable. He could not see Ben stringing her along and then cruelly dropping her when he tired of her company. Ben would not be that sort.

Shawn caught at his thoughts, stirred restlessly. How could he be so certain? He didn't think Ben was guilty of taking twenty thousand dollars' worth of gold that had been entrusted to him either, but there was every indication that he had. When it came down to facts, he really knew absolutely nothing about the Ben of today — only about the Ben of ten years and more ago when they were small boys on a farm in Ohio.

"You're finding it hard to believe Damon could steal — and murder," Cassie said, reading his thoughts.

"Not sure he did," he replied stubbornly.

She smiled. "That's just what I mean. You can't accept it. Why not? He's like any other man, has the same wants and needs — and like other men, satisfies them the best way he can."

Shawn shrugged. "He was brought up not to look at things that way. Can't see him forgetting it."

"People can change. Bad luck, hard times, other people force them to. Believe me, I know."

"Expect you're right, but until I hear him admit it, I'll keep on thinking it was somebody else. . . . Time we moved on."

Cassie rose, started toward the mare. "I think I feel sorry for you," she said hesitantly. "There's such a thing as too much faith. I know — I've been down that road, too. But you wake up, and you realize that people are what they are — not what you want them to be. It's a hard bump to take when it comes."

Starbuck had crossed to the waiting horses

with her; now, hand on her elbow he assisted her to mount. Thoughtful, he turned to the sorrel, swung onto the saddle. She was right, he had to admit; he'd knocked around, seen enough of life to know she spoke the truth. Yet, where Ben was concerned, there was a difference. . . . He was certain of it.

They rode on, keeping to the foot of the low, sprawling mountains, taking advantage of the infrequent shade as much as possible. Late in the afternoon they crossed a small creek; halted long enough to refresh themselves, water the horses, and fill the canteens; and then pressed on.

"Can't we camp here for tonight?" Cassie wondered. She was showing the strain of the long day of continual traveling.

"Good three hours more until dark," Starbuck responded. "Best we cover as much ground as we can before then."

She nodded woodenly. The trail, so faint it was barely discernible, continued to wind through the mesquite, scatters of storm-displaced rocks, rabbitbush, and other growth. Only here and there a paloverde or a lonely ironwood broke the sameness of a land so desolate it seemed they were the only living things. But he knew such was far from the fact; because of its isolation, it was a favored area for prowling Indians and Mexican bandits, and he had long since sharpened his vigilance.

This paid off abruptly. Motion on the side of the hill caught his attention. He halted immediately, caught at the black's reins as the girl moved up beside him.

"What is it?" she asked, voice going tense when she saw his face.

"Indians," he replied. "On the slope above us. Don't think they've spotted us yet."

She followed his gaze. "I see them. . . . Six . . . no seven," she said in a low voice. "They're watching something behind us."

"Hunting party, more than likely. Could be a deer they're looking at."

"What can we do?"

He brought his attention back to the trail. They were at the edge of a small clearing. On the opposite side there was a rocky butte gashed by a fair-sized arroyo.

"Hide — in there," he said, pointing. "With a little luck they'll override us. Come on."

He guided the sorrel to the butte, keeping well in the brush that fringed the clearing. Cassie followed close behind, the mare crowding the gelding's hindquarters all the way. When they reached the wash, both dismounted hurriedly, and Starbuck, taking the reins of both horses, led them in under a mesquite, where they would not be noticed, and doubled back quietly to where Cassie huddled beside a large rock.

"Stay here," he said, whispering. "I'll crawl up on top. Think I can watch them from there. Soon as they've passed, we'll get out of here — fast. Main thing, don't move around, and don't make any noise."

23

Moving silently, Starbuck climbed the slight grade behind the clearing, making good use of the dense brush. Moments later he reached the crest of the butte, halted. Flat on his belly, he studied the braves. They were little more than fifty yards distant, riding parallel to the meadow below, their lean, wiry ponies picking a trail through the rocks and springy growth. It was apparent the Apaches were also taking pains to travel quietly.

He glanced down. Cassie was still crouched next to the boulder where he had last seen her. Her features were strained, and several times she brushed nervously at her eyes. Beyond her the horses were barely distinguishable under the thorny mesquite. Only sudden movement on their part, or its resulting racket, would reveal them to the braves.

He gave thought as to what he should do

if for some reason the Apaches decided to ride off the slope and enter the clearing. At that level they would immediately see the girl and the horses. He had an ideal location, since he would be above them and could have them under his gun at all times. The problem would be to warn Cassie, tell her to pull back farther into the wash without betraying his position.

Brushing at the sweat clouding his vision, he continued to watch the braves, and then he heaved a sigh of relief. The Apaches appeared to have no intention of swerving from the course they were taking. Lithe, half-bent, coppery shapes on their ponies, they were intent only on whatever it was farther on that was holding their attention. He wondered what it could be — a deer, as he had thought, or some pilgrim taking the shorter way to Tucson?

"Cassie . . ."

At the sharp call, Starbuck twisted about, looked down into the little meadow below. A rider moved out from the far side of the brush, halted in the open. He stirred wearily. It was John Truxton. And then, as the girl came to her feet, Shawn threw a worried look at the Apaches. They had stopped, appeared to be listening. It came to him at once. It had been Truxton they were moving in on, and they now had lost sight of the man.

Starbuck frowned. If the mining foreman raised his voice again, he'd give them all away to the braves, but Shawn couldn't risk calling out. That would have the same result. Twisting about, he began a slow, careful retreat.

"I'm not letting you leave me," he heard Truxton say in a normal tone.

"You can't stop me this time, John," Cassie replied, keeping her voice down. "I won't go back. You can't make me."

"It'll be different now, I promise you. I've quit the mine. We'll move to some big town, like you've always wanted to do. . . . We're rich, Cassie. You didn't know that."

"Rich!" she scoffed. "A few dollars — that's what you call rich. I'm going to Damon. He's the one that's rich, and I . . . I love him."

Truxton had dismounted, was standing near the center of the clearing. Starbuck, pausing to look, saw the pack mule he was trailing for the first time. Evidently the foreman had left Skull, was willing to do anything that would please the girl.

"He's not rich, Cassie. . . ."

Shawn switched his eyes to the Apaches. They were still halted on the slope, puzzled by their inability to hear the sound of Truxton's passage. So far the conversation taking place in the clearing had not reached them.

"How do you know?"

At Cassie's question Starbuck brought his attention back to the pair below. He'd best keep moving, get to where he could warn them about the Apaches. Seemingly, Cassie had forgotten all about the danger.

"I know," Truxton said, and pointed to the loaded mule. "I've got over thirty thousand dollars' worth of gold there, Cassie. Think of it — thirty thousand dollars' worth! We can go anywhere you want, live like a king and queen!"

Shawn had paused in his slow descent, was staring at Truxton. Cassie, too, was regarding the man with surprise and suspicion.

"I don't believe you. . . . Where would you get that much?"

John Truxton laughed. "From Skull, where else? Some I saved up from what I was paid —"

"Not thirty thou—"

"Naw, only a part. But there's plenty of ways to build up a pile. Was always able to siphon off a little, take myself a little cut — and that there twenty thousand dollars' worth that Damon Friend took . . . ?"

Tense, Starbuck waited for the man to continue. Cassie took a step toward her husband.

"What about it?" she pressed in a tight voice.

"Wasn't him that got it, so if you're running to him because you think he's rich, better forget it. That gold's right there on my pack mule. . . . Friend's busted flat, same as he always was and always will be."

Cassie was staring at him. "That's a lie!"

"The gospel truth, every bit of it. I worked the whole kit and kaboodle. Sent him to town with the shipment, then took it away from him."

"I won't believe it! Damon wouldn't've let you take it away from him — and he wouldn't have just rode out."

Truxton smiled knowingly. "That there part was easy — mighty easy, thanks to you. Anyways, now we're all set. Nix sent me to Tucson to get Friend arrested. We're heading east instead. Be a week before anybody knows we're gone."

Shawn, hunched behind a clump of oak brush, listened intently. Satisfaction and relief were coursing through him in a clean, clear wave as the truth unfolded before him. He had been right about Ben. Truxton had framed him.

Just how the crusher foreman had managed it all was yet to be learned, but that would come shortly, Shawn decided grimly — just as soon as he could get off the butte's slope and face Truxton, Apaches permitting.

"Reckon you can see now you'd be a fool to leave me for him," the mining man continued. "It's me that's rich, not him. I'm the one that can give you everything you want."

The girl stirred indifferently. "It doesn't matter, John. The gold, I mean. You've got to understand that. I'm going to him anyway."

Truxton took an involuntary step forward. His hard face took on a dark frown. "Always thought it was money that counted with you. Money and living high and having things."

"I guess it was, once. Not anymore. Even so, I won't live with you, John. I couldn't stand it."

He swore savagely. "I'm warning you, Cassie! It's me or nobody!" he shouted.

Starbuck froze, flung a glance at the Apaches. They had heard — or thought they had heard — something, were looking in the direction of the clearing. At once he crawled to the edge of the brush.

"Keep your voice down!" he called hoarsely to Truxton. "Apaches!"

The foreman's eyes flared with surprise. "You!" he snapped, looking up at Shawn. "Figured all along you'd be helping her!"

"Something we'll all need if you don't ease off. There's seven Apaches over there on that slope that've been closing in on you. Right now they're not sure where you are, but you keep yelling and you'll have them down on us."

"The hell with them!" Truxton snarled. "The hell with everything!" Face dark, mouth working convulsively, he wheeled to Cassie. "Giving you your last chance. You're coming with me!"

"No, not this time."

"This time's no different than the others. You're mine, and I ain't letting nobody —"

"It is different, John. You've got to understand that."

"Understand — no! If I can't have you, nobody can!" Truxton shouted, and drawing his pistol, fired point-blank at the girl.

216

24

Cassie jolted as the heavy slug smashed into her, knocked her back into the brush. Starbuck, shocked by Truxton's sudden and unexpected move, stared at the man for a long breath; and then, as the sudden hammer of hooves on the slope warned him that the Apaches had heard, were racing in, he leaped from the rim of the low butte into the clearing.

"In here!" he shouted at the mining foreman, standing transfixed in the center of the open ground. Smoke was still trickling from the barrel of the weapon he held.

Shawn bent down, grasped Cassie by the shoulders, and dragged her deeper into the brush. She was dead; there was no doubt of that. Yells were coming from the hillside to the left and from farther to the right. The braves had split, were rushing in from two sides. Starbuck glanced anxiously at Truxton. He had not moved, seemed paralyzed.

"Come on!" he shouted.

In almost the same instant, gunshots echoed through the hills. Dirt erupted in the clearing around the foreman's feet. The Apaches were opening up on him, their only visible target. Truxton awoke from his torpor, seemingly jarred back to consciousness by the shooting. He looked wildly about, started toward Starbuck, concealed in the brush, at a lunging run. He covered two strides, staggered as bullets drove into him, regained his balance, and came on.

"I'm hit!" he gasped, and fell forward, half in, half out of the brush.

Starbuck caught him by the arms, pulled him into shelter. He gave the man a critical glance. There were two wounds in his body. He would be of no help in fighting off the Apaches.

Taut, Shawn wrenched the pistol from Truxton's nerveless fingers; hunched low, he moved to his left, where a fair-sized boulder offered protection. Then, a weapon in each hand, he waited for the Apaches.

They came at a rush, some racing in from the lower end of the clearing, the remainder from the opposite side. Starbuck, resting the pistols on the top of the rock, fired the weapon in his left hand at one group, challenged the other with his right.

Two of the braves buckled, fell from their ponies. Shawn got another as they wheeled away. He had taken them by surprise; apparently they were unaware of his presence, had thought they were dealing only with Truxton.

A deep silence fell over the clearing. Wisps of smoke and the dead Apaches were the only evidence of the violence that had transpired in so brief a time. But it was far from over, Starbuck knew, and hurried to reload.

"They . . . gone . . . ?"

Truxton's voice was low, the words dragging.

"Only long enough to think it over. They'll try again."

There was a short silence. Then, "Cassie — she dead?"

"Yes."

Truxton sighed heavily. "Suppose I ought to be sorry I done it, but I ain't. She was my woman — wife. Just couldn't stand for nobody else having her."

"You fixed it for both of you," Starbuck said unfeelingly.

"Guess so, but maybe if there's a hereafter we can get together — if she'll forgive me. . . . You figure there's a chance?"

"Something I'd not even try to guess,"

219

Shawn said, eyes sweeping back and forth over the clearing. There was no sign of the Apaches. "Want to ask you something."

"Best you hurry. . . ."

"Damon Friend's my brother. You said —"

"Your brother?"

"Yeh. Said you'd taken that gold away from him. Little hard to believe you could do that without a fight."

"Was easy. Sent him to town with it. Was to be alone, but that damned Jamie hitched himself a ride. Had to kill him so's he wouldn't talk."

"Thought I was told that taking that shipment in alone was my brother's idea."

"What I made others believe," Truxton said, and paused. A spasm of coughing seized him. When it had passed, he swore feebly, said, "Reckon I'm about due."

Shawn looked at the man closely. His dark skin had grayed, and a dull luster filled his eyes. "The gold — how'd you get it away from Ben — Damon Friend — and make it look like he'd run off with it?"

"Oh . . . that. Went on ahead of him . . . without him knowing. Got his horse, met him outside of town." Truxton's voice was low and his words came with difficulty.

"Acted . . . real mad. Told him I . . . was firing him because . . . because he was carrying on . . . with Cassie. Said I'd kill . . . her unless . . . he got on . . . his horse . . . left the . . . country."

The long speech had exhausted the mine foreman. He lay back, breath coming in short, wheezing gasps. It was all so simple once it was told, Shawn thought, yet so damaging to Ben when not explained.

"If you . . . you see . . . your brother . . . tell him . . ."

The clearing suddenly erupted again with a flurry of shots and thudding of hooves. Bullets smacked into the rock behind which Starbuck crouched, glanced off into space. Others clipped through the brush, buried themselves in the soil. Again steadying the brace of pistols on the boulder, Shawn waited until the quartet of braves reached the center of the open ground, and then began to trigger his weapons.

The Apache in the lead threw up his arms, went backward off his pony. The one next to him clutched at his leg, curved off to the side. The two remaining hauled up abruptly, and as Starbuck opened up again, they wheeled, followed their wounded comrade into the brush.

Reloading again, Shawn listened intently. For a time there was only the hush born of the shooting, and then in the distance he heard gravel spilling down the slope. The Apaches had given it up. Sighing, Shawn holstered his weapon, thrust the other pistol under his belt, and turned to Truxton.

"I'll see what I can do about those bullet-holes," he said, bending over the man. "Might be able to get you back to Wicken-burg in time for . . ."

He let the words trail off. There was nothing he or anyone else could do for John Truxton. What remained now was to get the bodies of Cassie and the crusher foreman back to the settlement, along with the gold being carried by the mule, repeat Truxton's account of what he had done, and then head for Tucson. . . . Ben had been there. Perhaps he still was.

ABOUT THE AUTHOR

Ray Hogan was born in Missouri in 1918. Married, with two children, he has lived most of his life in New Mexico. His father was an early Western marshal and lawman, and Hogan himself has spent a lifetime researching the West. In the last 30 years he has written over 200 articles and stories and 42 books, the majority dealing with the American West. His work has been filmed, televised, and translated into 6 languages.